in my Uncle's House

By Julie Nye

Bob Jones University Press, Greenville, South Carolina 29614

In My Uncle's House

Edited by Olivia Tschappler

Cover and illustrations by Stephanie True

© 1986 by Bob Jones University Press
Greenville, South Carolina 29614

ISBN 0-89084-349-X
Printed in the United States of America

20   19   18   17   16   15   14   13   12   11   10

To Ronda:
Without whose influence
I would never have been able to write
a story about surrender to God

Contents

CHAPTER ONE
CONFRONTATION

Travis McLarren lay perfectly still. So still that he could have been one of the large craggy rocks that dotted the windswept hillside. Chin on hands, he lay prone, almost hidden in the tall, tan grass of late summer.

A scant foot before him, two mounds of freshly turned soil interrupted the dry grass. Atop the mounds, amidst a circling of wild roses, lay a freshly cut stone. The boy's eyes were fixed on the words engraved on the stone. The words read, *Together Forever—Travis McLarren, Sr., and Grace Shelver McLarren.*

Some distance to the side lay two other stones. The larger, flat and plain, was engraved *James McLarren III; b. 1885, Scotland—d. 1967, Kentucky.* The smaller was elaborately cut, carved with flowers, vines, and a tiny Bible. On it were the words *Annie Dainler McLarren.* The tangled grass hid the old stones completely, but Travis knew they were there.

Nearby, at the edge of a grove of poplars, a mare stood tethered to a tree. She tossed her black mane and blew gently, looking toward the boy lying in the grass. Farther down the hill a tricolored foxhound cast back and forth at a run, his nose close to the ground. Giving up his quest for fresh scent, he trotted back to the boy.

Whining, the dog snuffled at the boy's dark red hair. Getting no response, he sat down to scratch energetically at a flea. Finishing his exhausting effort, he followed Travis's example and flopped in the grass. With a final noisy sigh, he was still.

An indefinite period of time passed before the dog sat up, ears perked. Travis glanced at the mare. She had turned her head as far as the tether would permit. Both dog and horse looked toward the crest of the hill. A few seconds later Travis heard the faint rumble of a car passing over a plank bridge. At that, the hound leaped straight into the air, splitting the silence with a drawn-out bay. He took off running. Travis, already on his feet and running toward the mare, shouted to the dog, "Buck! Over here!"

Travis pulled the mare's reins loose and vaulted into the saddle. Whirling her around, he sent her up the hill in plunging bounds. The dog half-circled and ran behind. On the way down the other side, Travis recklessly urged the mare to full speed on the shortest path to the house. The mare dug in, ears flattened, and tore across the field. Scruffy heifers scattered, bawling in panic as the horse and the dog charged through their midst.

Moments later, Travis reined in the horse midway down their long drive. A large barn and several small outbuildings stood behind him, and a grayed frame house to his right. A dark blue car jolted slowly up the rough road. Travis heard a screen door creak open, then slam shut. He knew his sisters, Laurie and Dana, stood on the porch, but not even Laurie's soft call made him turn to look. All his attention was fixed on the approaching car.

The mare spun and reared as the driver blew the horn. Travis jerked his horse around again with unusual roughness. She stood, eyes rolling as she picked up his tension.

The car stopped twenty feet from the horse. The driver stuck his head out of the window. The afternoon sun glinted off his dark glasses and picked out the silver in his black hair. "How about letting us by, Travis?" he called.

Travis's retort came swiftly. "You're far enough."

Scowling, the man withdrew his head. A moment later the engine cut and two men emerged.

Both men wore flawless business suits that seemed absurdly out of place against the backdrop of rocky fields, green-wooded mountains, and smoky-blue peaks.

The taller of the men reached toward Buck, who was sniffing suspiciously in their direction. "Hi, boy," he said. Buck leaped away, letting out another series of earsplitting bays.

A shrill whistle pierced the din. The noise stopped. Buck turned, dashing to a thin girl in a cotton dress and pigtails who stood on the porch. The man approached Travis's horse, which backed away a step.

"Winsome doesn't like strangers either." Travis's voice was flat.

"Hello, Travis, it's good to see you again, too," the man said with a twist to his mouth.

"What do you want, Mr. Shelver?"

"Mr. Shelver? Really, Travis, I *am* your uncle." Getting no reply, he continued. "Didn't you get our letter? We'd like to talk to you and your sisters, but it's kind of hard with you up there."

"We?"

"My attorney, Mr. Evans," he indicated the man behind him.

"We have some papers concerning your parents," Mr. Evans said as he came forward. "We thought you might be interested."

Travis touched the mare lightly and cantered to the house. He dropped the reins as he dismounted. Ignoring the steps, he jumped up onto the porch beside his sisters. "Laurie, don't listen to him," he pleaded. "Send him packin'!"

"Why, Travis?" Dana looked up, both hands still fastened firmly on Buck's collar. "Do they still want to make us leave?"

"Hush, Dana, we'll all know soon enough," the older girl said. The two younger children stood on either side of Laurie as the two men approached. The light breeze blew thin strands of red hair across Laurie's face, emphasizing her tired expression. She rubbed her hands nervously on the oversized apron she wore, brushing off traces of flour where she had hastily wiped her hands. "Travis," she murmured, "I don't really think there's anything we can do. None of us is of age."

"Shh!" he said sharply as the men reached the porch.

"Hello, Laurie, Dana," their uncle said.

Dana said nothing, but her eyes were bright and curious.

"Hello, Uncle Wade," Laurie answered. "How are you?"

"Just fine, Laurie. I'd like you to meet Mr. Phillip Evans, my attorney and also the appointed officer of the probate court. Phillip, this is Laurie McLarren, her sister, Dana, and you've met Travis."

"How do you do, Mr. Evans?" Laurie stepped forward with her hand extended. He reached out and shook it, looking her over thoroughly.

"Very well, thank you. It's a pleasure meeting you." He paused and stepped back. "We have some things to discuss. Do you suppose we could go inside?"

"Certainly," Laurie said graciously. She motioned them ahead of her to the door, ignoring Travis's black glare.

Some time later all five were still gathered in the living room. Wade Shelver and Phillip Evans lounged in chairs. Travis stood with his back to the others, staring out the window. Once he looked at Dana out of the corner of his eye. A ghost of a smile passed quickly across his face as he saw her sitting cross-legged by the empty fireplace. She had pointedly ignored all her uncle's attempts to talk to her. She sat holding one of her favorite books, keeping herself aloof with an air of rigid disapproval. Then Travis's frown returned as he heard Laurie speak from her seat on the edge of the sofa.

"So, Mr. Evans," she said, her voice shaking slightly before she steadied it. "Let me get this straight. The bonds, which were to have been mine and Dana's, must go to cover the taxes and to pay off the mortgage."

"Correct. And even then they won't cover it all."

"So the farm is to pass into Travis's name when he turns eighteen, which won't happen for more than three years. Meanwhile, Uncle Wade is our legal guardian—as well as having jurisdiction over the farm?"

"Yes. Since your father's brother mentioned in your parents' will has been presumed dead for the last six years, the court has named Wade Shelver as your guardian."

"And at your suggestion, Uncle Wade has decided that the farm must be sold to finish paying the mortgage?"

"There's no need to leave outstanding debts. And without income there is no way of paying the yearly taxes. We've already negotiated with an agency that is very interested in opening a resort in this area. The bills will be paid and a tidy profit put into your estate fund."

"A resort!" Travis cut in. "RESORT!" Though Mr. Evans glared at him, Travis continued. "What happens if we don't like your decision?"

Wade Shelver took his cue. "It has already been contested by the district attorney, who felt that you should have the right to choose whether the farm should be sold." Their uncle stared at the arm of his chair, where he tapped his fingers lightly. "However, since there was no clause in your parents' will specifically stating that the farm wasn't to be sold, we were able to have the protest overruled."

Travis turned back to the window. Laurie pushed her auburn hair back from her face. "Uncle Wade, isn't there any possible way that we can renew the mortgage or something? Can't we at least stay here and try to make it work? Surely you realize that Mom and Dad intended for us to keep the property."

Mr. Evans raised his eyebrows. "Three children running a farm? Alone? Preposterous!"

"He's right. Staying here during the summer is one thing—trying to run a farm and attend school is another." Wade stood up. Looking directly at Laurie, he said firmly, "But that, Laurie, is not the point. The point is that I have been given the authority to make the decision. I am legal guardian of all three of you, in addition to being trustee of the estate, which you are not entitled to receive until you come of age!"

For a moment he studied an old photograph of Travis and Grace McLarren that had been taken shortly after their marriage. Turning back, he leaned on the wall beside the picture. "Furthermore, the sales arrangements have already been finalized. The agency will be here to take possession of the place in ten days."

Travis jerked around from the window again. Everyone stiffened, expecting another outburst. But Travis only walked slowly and deliberately toward Wade until he stood barely two feet away. Looking up slightly to stare the man in the eye, Travis spoke in a voice that contrasted oddly with the image of a fourteen-year-old.

"I finally think I get it. Why Dad never liked to discuss you and your family. You think we're a bunch of ignorant hillbillies, don't you? Well, I know about you and your kind. I know the way you operate. It wouldn't ruffle the fringe on your pockets to let this farm go for three years, but how many thousands will you make from the deal, Uncle Wade? Will we ever see a penny of the money?"

"I have made what I consider to be the decision in the best possible interests of all concerned." Wade's voice was low and furious.

"Our best interests! That's really good! I think it would have been in our better interests if you had been in Merlana Gap, instead of Mom and Dad, when that tornado went through!"

"Travis!" Laurie's voice was sharp and fearful, but she didn't continue. Travis and his uncle remained in an eye-to-eye stare-down. Wade looked away first. He pivoted on his heel, then stopped at the door. Looking back at the two older children, he said, "We'll be back a week from today. I'll send a van for anything you want to keep and put in storage. You'll be coming to Asheville to stay in my house." He motioned to Mr. Evans, the door shut, and they were gone.

None of the McLarrens moved until the sound of the car's engine slowly faded away. Then Laurie moved to the kitchen alcove. "I guess we've got a lot to do," she said.

"Laurie!" The single word was an accusation. "We can't just let them get away with this! This was our father's place, our grandfather's place!"

"There's nothing we can do to stop them. And Travis, you know God wouldn't let this happen to us unless He had a reason for it."

"God! That's all you talk about lately. I suppose you think He arranged for Mom and Dad's death, too!"

"He does have a better knowledge of our lives than we do, Travis. We'll never please Him, or be our best, unless we let Him work."

"I don't care about all that! I want to stay here!"

"Maybe He has something better for us—"

"I don't want anything else!" Travis was dangerously close to tears. "Laurie, I don't want to go!"

Laurie's strained temper broke. "Good grief, Travis! Grow up! Do you think I want to? What can I do? Throw a temper tantrum? Dig up a gold mine to buy Uncle Wade off and bribe the resort company? Produce a fairy godmother?"

Travis stepped back from her, his hand reaching out to grip the edge of a counter. "I won't go, Laurie. No one can make me. I can work for any one of a dozen men in the mountains. They'll never find me. Do you hear me? They can't stop me!"

"No, Travis." Laurie reached for a pan of bread dough. "No, they probably can't. But I have Dana to consider. And myself. So don't make it harder on us than it already is."

Her words struck Travis with an almost physical force. Dana. He had forgotten she was around. His eyes swung to her now as she stood, her fingers twisting one of her braids. Her freckles stood out on her white face as she silently watched the unusual strife between her brother and sister.

"It's your choice, Travis. I'm not going to try to make it for you," Laurie said, "but before you do anything, will you please make arrangements for the stock? They certainly can't stay on a resort."

The moment froze in time for Travis. He was to remember it for the rest of his life, in every detail. Laurie's rigid back as she kneaded the bread dough viciously; Dana's white face; the quaint old kitchen with its hardwood floor, red-checked curtains, and black stove; the ticking clock on the mantle; and the strong smell of fresh-cut dill lying in the sink.

A flash of red outside the window materialized into a cardinal. It sat on a branch, gently swaying up and down, and filled the silence with singsong chirping. The cheery notes drummed against Travis's head. "Quiet, bird," he thought. "Just be quiet!"

Heedless, the bird continued. Slowly the stiffness ebbed from Travis. He directed his barely audible answer to both sisters. "I'll be here. I guess I'd better get to the barn." Travis went out, the door slammed, and his boots clumped hollowly on the porch. Both girls watched him through the window as he picked up Winsome's trailing reins and led her towards the weather-beaten barn.

CHAPTER TWO
EMPTY FARM

"Go on, move!" Travis snapped at the balky heifer. Winsome pushed against it with her shoulder, and the heifer trotted reluctantly away to join the rest of the herd. Wiping his forehead, Travis stopped Winsome to let her rest. He scanned the surrounding hillside, then looked back toward the milling herd of cattle.

"Looks like we've about got the last of them, girl." Travis slapped the mare's sweaty shoulder gently. She snorted.

The afternoon sun slanted across the craggy hills, sending purple shadows down the valley. Travis ignored the rumble of his stomach as he sat staring down at the farm buildings scattered across the carpet of grass like a child's playthings. Unwillingly, his gaze traveled from his home, farther down the valley, to the jumble of destroyed buildings that used to be Merlana Gap. Travis's grip on the reins tightened as his eyes traced the ugly slash of wreckage that cut through the tiny town and slashed up the opposite mountainside. The tornado's sweep had been quick but merciless.

Winsome moved restlessly as the cattle began to drift. Travis signaled the mare to start pushing them southwest toward the river. The McLarren farm was bounded on the west side by a wide, deep river, and on the east by a section of the Smoky Mountains' highest, roughest heights. Many times over the years, when a round-up was required, Travis and his father had started at the northernmost part of the farm. They drove all cattle ahead of them until they reached the field where the river curved east to form the southern border of the farm. The resulting enclosure ranked second only to a box canyon for holding a herd. The only possible ford of the river lay right at its curve. Once across, the cattle were only yards from the road leading out of the mountains—easily available for truck loading and transfer.

Travis and Winsome had been doing double duty the last few days. All livestock had to be sold. Neighboring farmers had snapped up the choice cattle and the three other horses—Mr. McLarren's cow horse and the team of bays. This herd of cattle was the last. Trucks waited ahead to take them to the auction in the city.

A fringe of white birches separated the cattle from the last field before the ford. Travis had arranged for two horsemen to be waiting at the river to help, but the cattle would almost certainly try to make a break eastward when they came out of those trees.

"Come on, Winsome." Travis raised himself in the saddle briefly to stretch his cramped legs. "One more time, girl."

Yelling and waving his free arm, Travis ran the mare toward the rear of the herd. Used to such tactics, the cattle merely shook their heads and broke into a trot.

Counting on the herd's momentum, Travis swung Winsome east until she was clear of the cattle. Urging her into a hard run, he cut straight into the trees. Though tired, the little horse responded gamely, dodging branches and tree trunks and leaping windfalls in a fashion that would have ditched a rider less skilled than Travis.

Coming out of the fringe of trees, Travis noted with satisfaction that the herd had just appeared. As expected, they headed east immediately, but Winsome and Travis were already there. Bawling in annoyance, they turned toward the river again.

Nearly an hour later, Travis watched the cattle buyers slam the truck gate shut after the last cow. The muscles in his back ached, and his head throbbed.

"We thank you, son," said a leathery-faced man, coming up to Travis's side. "That's a right good haul, and we're sure glad to get 'em."

"Yeah, well," Travis rubbed his eyes clear of grit. "I'm sure sorry to see them go, but I can't do much about it."

"That's what I hear." The older man watched Travis intently for a moment. When no further reaction came, the man grunted and fished a check out of his pocket.

"Here ya go. That what we agreed on?"

Travis took the check. Glancing at it briefly, he nodded and stuffed it into his own pocket.

"Well, young McLarren." The man shook Travis's hand firmly. "Good luck to ya, wherever you're off to."

"Thanks," Travis said, doing his best to smile.

The cattle buyers climbed into their trucks. Motors ground, and the trucks started to roll away.

Travis felt his throat tighten as he watched them disappear down the winding road. When the low rumble of the trucks faded away completely, he turned Winsome down the road in the opposite direction. The black mare turned her head back toward the McLarren farm as they moved away.

"I know you want a good rest and feed," Travis told her. "And you'll get it."

He rode silently for a while; then, reaching forward to rub the horse's neck, he said huskily, "You know I can't take you with us, Winsome. You wouldn't like it. Dad always said that you were a working horse, not a pet. So I guess he would have left you here with the Rallerts, like I'm going to."

Winsome's ears tilted back slightly, listening to the boy on her back.

"That way you can still live the way you're used to living. Besides, the Rallerts need a good horse. Things haven't been real good for them lately."

They cut off the gravel road at an angle and jogged slowly toward a distant set of weathered buildings. "I know Mr. Rallert would've bought Dad's horse if he'd had the money. But you're just as good, and a lot younger, too."

As they approached a farmyard similar to their own, Travis fell silent. He stopped Winsome in front of the barn, but sat motionless, staring down at her for a long moment before dismounting. Three figures appeared from inside the barn.

"Hello, Travis," said the tallest one.

"Hello, Mr. Rallert, Dave, Jamie." Travis nodded at each one.

"We have her stall ready," Mr. Rallert continued. "Dave or Jamie will take care of her, if you like."

"Thanks, but I'd rather do it myself." Travis's smile was a little twisted. "They'll have plenty of chances to do it from now on, but. . . ."

"That's fine, son; you go ahead. You know where everything is anyway."

Travis unsaddled Winsome. Slowly and carefully he rubbed her down and brushed her until her black hide gleamed with a luster like mink. Then, he led her to the large box stall and turned her in. Grain, hay, and fresh water were laid out and waiting. Winsome wasted no time but plunged her nose right into the grain and started chomping noisily.

Travis leaned on the rough, wooden gate and watched as she cleaned the feed box of every last oat. Dave came up beside him. "I'll take good care of her, Travis, I promise."

"I know you will, Dave."

"Let me know your address. I'll write and tell you how she's doing."

"Okay." Travis felt a dangerous burning at the back of his eyes. The creak of the barn door told them Mr. Rallert was coming. Both boys turned to face him.

"Travis, I can't thank you enough for leaving Winsome with us. You could have gotten a good price for her."

"It's more important to me that I know you'll be good to her."

"Well, you have my word on that." Mr. Rallert cleared his throat and glanced at Winsome. "Travis, I couldn't begin to pay you what that mare is worth. So I'm not even going to try. I just wish I could think of a way." His voice drifted off for a moment. "Anyway," he continued, "you take care of yourself. And your sisters. We'll be praying for you."

Travis's face went blank. He turned back to Winsome's stall. Holding the last of his crumbled sugar lumps out to her, he watched the mare whisk them off his palm. Travis reached up and patted her. She stuck her head out the stall door, looked around, and whinnied.

"No, girl, you've got to stay here. You'll be better off." Travis put a hand on either side of her head for a moment, then turned and hurried away.

Mr. Rallert and Dave followed. "Can we give you a ride home?"

"Thanks, but I think I'd rather walk. I have time."

Travis shook hands with each in turn. "Good-bye. When I can get back this way, I'll stop by."

"Please do. Good-bye, Travis."

"Good-bye," echoed Dave.

"Wait," Jamie hurried up and handed him a loaf-sized package. "Mom fixed this for your supper. Tell Laurie good-bye for me."

Travis nodded. He took the loaf and started away. As he crossed the dirt drive, he heard a loud neigh from Winsome. Travis flinched but kept walking. The mare repeated her call.

Travis quickly lost the battle against tears, but he kept walking until he was sure he was out of sight of the farmyard. Then, breaking into a run, he did not stop until he neared his own home. Gasping for breath and sobbing uncontrollably, he threw himself against the solid trunk of a smooth white birch.

He clutched the trunk with both hands and held on until his sobs gradually died. Then, angrily wiping tears from his eyes, he looked across the plank bridge toward the farm that lay before him. It seemed strange and quiet— no cattle, no horses, no chickens, barn tightly shut.

The sun outlined the darkening peaks. Travis's gaze traveled across the slopes until it rested on one that was just north of the house.

"Dad," he whispered huskily. "I don't think I can do it. I just don't think I can do it."

Finally he pushed himself away from the tree and picked up Mrs. Rallert's gift. Then he squared his shoulders and started across the bridge that led to the house.

CHAPTER THREE

GOOD-BYE, MERLANA GAP

The next morning dawned clear, cool, and perfect. Travis stood on the porch in his stocking feet, surveying the mountains. Here and there, high up on the slopes, a few strokes of orange-yellow showed against the darker green of the trees. Frost had been to the higher country and would soon be in the valley. Travis felt strangely ill at ease. His eyes came to rest on the empty barn. On any other day, he would be down there finishing up the morning chores.

Buck bounded around the corner and leaped easily onto the porch. When Travis didn't seem to notice him, the big dog sat down and stared at the boy. Tilting his head to one side, he whined and scratched at Travis's leg with one paw.

Travis absently reached down and patted his head. Buck stood up and waved his tail happily. "Fine for you to be happy," Travis muttered at him. "If you only knew."

Buck whined again and snuffled at the air.

"I know what's on your mind," Travis told him. "The nip in the air means hunting time's on the way. You sure won't have any trouble adjusting to the life of a professional hound dog."

Travis had to smile. Buck would love being one of Jack Ferro's score of hounds. The man did nothing but train dogs and tramp the hills year-round, hunting for bounty.

"Travis!" Laurie's voice came out to him. "Are you going to eat breakfast or not?" Travis sighed, then turned and went inside. Sliding into his chair, he savored the aroma of eggs and sausage.

"I'll pray," Laurie said. They all bowed their heads as she spoke. "Lord, we commit this day to you, and we thank you for it. Help us as we leave today. We ask for your protection, and that we would be a good witness to Uncle Wade and to the rest of the family. Now bless this food. We pray in Christ's name. Amen."

Travis jerked his napkin from the table and unfolded it roughly. "Are you really glad to be leaving, Laurie?"

"No, Travis, I'm not. But like I've already said, God knows best for us. I'll thank Him for what He does, whether or not I understand it."

"You're crazy," was Travis's ungracious reply. "You can't name me one good thing about living with the Shelvers, and you know it."

"Travis!" Laurie's voice was strained.

Travis stabbed a piece of sausage and bit into it, instead of replying. He looked away from Laurie to the empty shelves and curtainless windows.

"Laurie?" Dana poked at her eggs. "Can't I at least ask Uncle Wade if we can take Buck?"

"No, Dana."

"Please? He's going to hate not being with us!"

"No, Dana, you can't. Mr. Ferro will be here any minute to get him. There's no way we could take a dog to Asheville."

"But—"

"Dana," Laurie said gently, leaning forward to brush the hair away from Dana's red-rimmed eyes. "Buck would be miserable there. Just as Winsome would have been. Think about what's best for him, not what you want."

"He'll hunt all the time, and you know how he loves to hunt," Travis said reassuringly. "If we took him with us, he'd probably be miserable."

Dana nodded silently, but her eyes stayed fixed on the table. All three concentrated on their breakfast.

"Can't you see, Travis, that what you just said is the way God works with us? We make the choice for Buck because we know better. Of course he would follow us if he had the choice. But we won't allow him to choose that because we know that in the long run, he'll be happier with Mr. Ferro."

Laurie stopped eating. Gripping her fork, she stared at Travis. "Can't you see that God can make that kind of a choice for us? He can see ahead. He knows what we need!"

"I'm not a dog, Laurie." Travis pushed his chair back and stood up. "All I know is that we're being forced to do something that is wrong. Wrong and unfair!"

"Okay, then." Laurie put her fork down on the table. "It's unfair. Even if it were downright illegal, can you take it? Do you have the guts and maturity to make the best of a bad situation?"

"Well, all you're doing is letting them push you around!" Travis spun on his heel and left the kitchen.

Laurie slumped in her chair. A hiccupping sound from Dana brought her attention back to the table. Though tears ran down her face, Dana tried to suppress her sobs.

"Dana, honey—"

"Everything is all wrong!" Dana choked out the words. "We have to leave. All you and Travis do anymore is fight!

Now you're giving Buck away. I'll probably be next! I want my mother!"

Her voice rising, Dana scrambled from her chair and fled. Outside a horn blew, setting off a frenzy of baying. Laurie sent an exasperated look to the ceiling and started to clear the table.

Travis, after exchanging greetings with Jack Ferro, leaned against the cab of the ancient truck. Both watched Buck. Stiff-legged, the big foxhound approached. He circled the truck once. The dozen hounds in the truck bayed anxiously, but were too well trained to get out. Buck stopped and looked quizzically at Travis.

"It's okay," Travis told him. "You leave them alone, got it?" Buck sat down and waited.

Jack Ferro climbed out of the cab. With one eye on Buck, and the other on his own dogs, the man spoke loudly. "Rouster! Hey, Rouster! Here!"

A huge black and tan Walker hound pushed through the squirming, yelping pack and leaped to the ground.

The nearby foxhound jumped up, bristling. "Buck!" Travis stamped his foot sharply. Buck subsided.

"Rouster's my lead dog," Ferro said.

Travis nodded. If the lead dog accepted Buck, so would the rest of the pack.

The dogs approached each other stiffly. The two owners watched anxiously until, inspection over, the dogs settled down.

Travis turned to Jack Ferro. "You'll be good to him, won't you?"

"Yeah, you better believe it. He's a good dog." The man held out his fingers to Buck, who sniffed them with interest. "Don't you kids worry about him. I won't sell him off, and if you ever want him back, just say so."

Travis nodded, and they shook hands. Dana had been standing quietly on the porch, tear stains evident. Now she came slowly forward and threw her arms around Buck. Buck whined and tried to lick her face.

"Well, luck to you, kid," Ferro said awkwardly, snapping his fingers at Rouster. The big Walker followed him to the tailgate, and then jumped in as Ferro opened it.

"Go on, Buck," Travis encouraged. "Go on!" Buck followed the other dog to the tailgate, and then hesitated. "That's it," Travis went and patted his head. "Get up, boy. You go too." Travis waved him ahead. Buck jumped into the truck. Immediately he was submerged by curious hounds and waving tails.

Travis stepped back and put his arm around Dana. Ferro climbed back in his cab and started the truck down the driveway. Travis waved, and Ferro tooted his horn in response, starting off another session of baying from the back. At the bridge, Ferro pulled aside to let a car and a large van pass.

Laurie came out to stand beside the other two as the car led the van, bouncing and swaying, up the deeply rutted drive. A moment later the engines cut, doors opened, and Wade Shelver's voice could be heard speaking to two other men."You get the van open. I'll go make sure they're ready."

He came to the porch with a bold stride. Nodding briefly at Travis, Wade directed his question to Laurie."Is everything all set?"

"I guess we're as ready as we'll ever be." The flatness of Laurie's tone jerked Travis's attention to her face. She looked tired and spent.

Travis leaped up on the porch and placed himself almost between his sister and his uncle. Wade gave him a measuring look, then spoke. "Well, let's get started. There's a long drive ahead of us."

Travis would remember that morning for the rest of his life. Laurie hurried quietly about, doing last-minute odds and ends. Travis and the two moving men went back and forth in the loading process. Dana sat on the edge of the porch, huddled beside the box that contained her books, the doll her mother had made last year for her seventh birthday, and a few other treasures from the fields and woods around their home. Wade Shelver moved back and forth, stony-faced, trying to stay aware of everything that happened.

The morning faded into afternoon before they finished. Wade took their bags outside to put them in his car and to give final instructions to the men in the van, who would be going on ahead of them to Asheville.

Travis, Laurie, and Dana were left alone in the stripped and empty house. "Go around and check everywhere," Laurie instructed. "Make sure we're not leaving anything. Travis, you take the upstairs. Dana, you look in the basement. I'll check around here."

Travis went up the stairs three at a time. Moving as quickly as possible, he walked through the rooms, a lump growing bigger and bigger in his throat. The bare boards creaked under his feet, and when he stood still, he could hear the echoing clatter of his sister's movements below.

When he touched the brass knob on the door to his parents' room, the door swung open gently. Light from the curtainless windows poured into every corner, exposing the raw emptiness of the room. Trying to quiet his heavy boots, the boy walked across to the window. He leaned his head against the warm panes and looked down. The weathered farm buildings nestled into the slope, neat fences corralled the dry grass of summer, and the old barn stood guard over all. The familiar surroundings blurred, and he blinked hard. A spider ran over his hand, startling him.

Angrily, he dashed the spider away and tore down the web it had begun to spin. He left the room and closed the door firmly.

Then he stomped down the stairs, making as much noise as possible. In the hall, he found Laurie, arms around Dana.

"Listen!" Laurie grabbed one of each of their hands and squeezed them fiercely. "We're going to make it! We're going to stick together and we're going to be all right!"

"What's going on in there?" Wade's voice shouted from outside. "Are you ready to go?"

"Let's pray." Laurie's voice was a quick whisper. "Dear God," she began as Wade came through the door and stopped short at the sight of their little circle. "Keep us safe, keep us right, keep us close to You. We ask for your guidance. And Lord, please, help us not to be afraid. In the name of our Lord Jesus Christ. Amen."

Laurie turned to Wade. "Yes, sir, we're ready."

Their footsteps echoed hollowly on the floor as they walked out. Travis pulled the door shut, and the lock turned with a quiet click.

Moments later, they were inside the big car, bumping down the driveway. Travis looked over his shoulder and the tightness in his chest threatened to cut off his breath.

"Don't look back," Laurie said quietly. Travis hesitated a moment, then turned around, leaned back, and closed his eyes.

CHAPTER FOUR
CHELLAVUE

Travis had never known houses were built so big. He stared in amazement as they turned onto a blacktopped driveway. To the right of the drive began a series of white-fenced paddocks. An occasional horse grazed in a paddock, but Travis's gaze remained riveted to the house on the left. Mammoth and white, it stood under a graceful canopy of huge shade trees. Gleaming pillars, lined up on a brick porch, supported a second-floor veranda. On either side, modern additions blended with the graceful architecture of days long gone.

Wade Shelver raised his eyebrows at the incredulous looks on all three faces. "Didn't your mother ever show you pictures of Chellavue?" he asked.

"We've seen pictures of people, and of parts of different rooms," Laurie answered. "But I never knew, I mean, I knew it was nice, but no, we've never seen pictures of the whole house."

"Hmmph." Wade's reply was noncommittal. "Well, Edward Shelton had it built in 1847. Used to be the manor house of a cotton plantation."

Wade stopped the car before the house. The brick porch ran the entire length of the house, underlining the large, imposing door and windows. Travis climbed stiffly out of the car, then opened the door for Laurie and Dana. He lifted out Dana's box and then reached into the back for the bags.

"Leave your things," Wade said, glancing at his watch impatiently. "They will be taken to your rooms for you. Now, let's go. You need to meet the family, and dinner will be in less than an hour."

Wade started across the bricks toward the door. Dana gave Travis an anguished look, and then clutched her box firmly. Travis looked at Laurie and shrugged his shoulders. "Let her keep it," he said.

At the door Wade gave Dana an exasperated glance. She looked back unyieldingly, holding the box in front of her. Before he could say anything, the door opened.

Travis stopped short as a slightly-built, dark-haired woman appeared in the doorway. He heard Laurie's soft intake of breath behind him. Everyone stood still for a moment. Wade's eyes glanced quickly around at all present. Then Dana spoke in a loud whisper. "Laurie, that's Mom's sister, isn't it?"

The woman smiled and came forward. Kneeling on the bricks in front of Dana, she took the box and set it down. "Yes, honey, I sure am. And I am just delighted to see you!"

Dana's face broke into a tremulous smile, and she leaned into the woman's arms. Travis, still marveling at the woman's striking resemblance to his mother, knew that Dana had just been won over. He hardly realized that the woman had risen and introduced herself by a familiar name.

"I'm Emily Shelver. And you must be Travis, and Laurie, and of course, you're Dana."

Wade cut in. "Emily, where is Catherine?"

"She's in the study. Some last-minute work on the hospital project, I'm sure."

Wade's lips thinned as he spun on his heel. "Come on. Everyone!"

Emily Shelver took Dana's hand and led her after Wade. Laurie and Travis exchanged brief, apprehensive glances, and then followed.

As they stepped through the huge doorway, the three young McLarrens hesitated. The large foyer arched up to a single high point, where a huge chandelier hung. Stairs rose in a high, gleaming curve toward the second floor. Brass-edged mirrors gleamed from the rich, textured finish of the walls.

Wade led them through a double doorway to the right. A fine Persian carpet almost covered the polished oak floors, accenting the dark antique desks that gleamed in the light from the French doors. At one of the desks, an immaculately groomed woman sat, speaking into a telephone.

Without putting down the telephone, she scrutinized each of the McLarrens thoroughly. Travis found it difficult to look back. By the time the receiver clicked back onto its hook, he felt squeezed and dirty.

"Laurie, Travis, Dana," Wade spoke in an even tone, "this is my wife, your Aunt Catherine."

"Hello," Dana and Laurie spoke together.

Travis remained silent.

Catherine Shelver rose suddenly, but with perfect grace. Her eyes flicked over their clothing with distaste and rested on Dana's box. "I hope you had a good trip. I'm sure you must be tired. I'll have one of the servants show you to your rooms so that you can freshen up and change for dinner."

"Catherine!" Wade's voice was taut.

Ignoring him, Catherine stepped toward the door. Emily intercepted her, meeting her sister-in-law's eyes calmly. "Never mind, Catherine. I'll take them up."

"If you wish," Catherine replied indifferently. "Dinner will be in half an hour then."

Letting out his breath wearily, Wade dropped into the chair behind the other desk. Travis gave him a long look, and then turned and followed the others.

Dana relinquished her box to Emily and ran quickly to the landing. She waited for the others with a delighted grin. "Is this where Mom fell over the railing when she was little?"

"Um-hm," Emily nodded, "and your uncle fell over there three or four times, I think."

On the second floor she led them down a long, wide hall. Pictures of hunting dogs and prize-winning show horses lined the hallway. Each picture carried a brass plate on the frame. Without displaying an obvious interest, Travis was able to pick out the name "Chellavue" on almost every plate.

Back to the right, past five or six doors, she stopped and opened a door. "This will be your room, Travis. Your sisters will be in the next two rooms down on the same side of the hall."

Travis glanced at her suspiciously. "This place is a hotel," he muttered.

Emily's answering laugh surprised him. "Yes, it is. Give me a cottage any day. But you'll get used to it." The smile on her face was suppressed, but her eyes still laughed. "You go on now. Your things are already there. Meet me back at the stairs in a few minutes and I'll take you to the dining room."

Travis pushed the door the rest of the way open. Stepping in, he swung it shut. Bold, blue plaid leaped out at him from the drapes, the chair, and the bedspread. Deep mahogany woodwork emphasized the dark plush of the blue carpeting. His incredulous gaze took in the large desk, the spacious shelves, the chair by the doors, and the huge dresser. Light from the glass-paned doors that opened out onto the veranda glinted off every polished surface.

Travis sat down on the corner of the bed, staring at the blessedly familiar, battered old suitcases standing in the middle of the floor. "Never!" he muttered. "Never in my life. . . ."

Sharp, angry voices penetrated his thoughts. Travis's head jerked up, startled. It took only a moment to pinpoint the source of the voices. They came through the slightly open doors. He went to the doors and pushed them the rest of the way open. Only then did he realize that his room must be almost directly over the study. He could hear Catherine Shelver's high voice clearly.

"Emily, I think you are being more than unreasonable. All this maudlin sentiment is enough to make me sick!"

"Catherine, they are Grace's children!" Emily's low reply was barely audible. "Doesn't that mean anything to you?"

"No! She never meant anything to me but trouble. I can't believe," Catherine went on, "that she was ever anything but grief to this family. I—"

"Enough!" Emily's voice rose sharply. "She was my sister, if you can bring yourself to remember!"

"So putting Laurie in her old room, when you've never let anyone else so much as breathe in there, is an attempt to prove your point?"

"I want to see that Travis and Grace's children are treated right—in spite of you."

Travis drew back inside, closing the door tightly to shut out the voices. He felt a little sick. Never before in his life had he heard such bitterness between two adults of a family. To quiet his thoughts, he went to the suitcases and began rummaging. He changed quickly and was putting some clothes in drawers when he heard hoof beats. Jumping up, he almost fell in his eagerness to get back out on the veranda.

On the way up to the house, he hadn't recognized the white fence about a hundred yards from the house as actually part of the pasture. Now a group of running horses, seven or eight strong, charged along the fence toward the house. Travis's admiring gaze was arrested by the blazing red chestnut in the lead. The big horse easily outdistanced the others. Swinging parallel to the fence, he pounded away with enormous strides. In a chorus of squeals and snorts, the others followed. Travis watched until they were out of sight. Then, going back inside, he slicked down his hair and went in search of the girls.

Two doors down the hall he hesitated and knocked softly. "Laurie?"

Dana's voice answered. "We're in here. Come on in."

He did and took a quick breath. "This was Mom's room when she was growing up?" He scanned the room full of delicate, French-styled furniture, trying to imagine his mother in such surroundings.

"Yes, but how did you know? Aunt Emily told us."

"I, well, overheard them talking. My room is right over the study."

Laurie gave him a questioning look, then resumed struggling with her hair. Anticipating a long wait, Travis said, "Don't you think we'd better get going? They probably have an execution penalty for being late."

"Oh!" Laurie gave her hair one last look and put the brush down. She surveyed his clothing carefully, then nodded. Smoothing Dana's collar, she pushed the girl gently toward the door and took a deep breath. "Okay, McLarrens, here we go!"

Halfway down the hall, they met Emily. "Good," she said, looking them over with satisfaction. "Now I'll try to help you make some sense from the layout of this house." She started down the stairs, and all three McLarrens trooped behind her. Emily stopped at the bottom.

"That way is the front door, the living room, and study—where you came in. Opposite is the den, the back veranda, and a reception parlor. Down that way, east, is the kitchen and dining rooms. Back this way is the library and some guest rooms."

She motioned them to follow her down a hall. "We'll be eating in the Garden Room tonight. It won't be too formal."

By whose standards? Travis thought as they entered an airy room filled with plants and framed by long windows that opened out onto a terrace. Near the windows a large, round table was set in fine linen, porcelain, and crystal. Wade, Catherine, and a small blonde girl stood waiting.

As the McLarrens walked across the tiled floor, Travis felt a sudden rush of gratitude to his mother. He'd often chafed under her persistent correction of table behavior, appearance, and general manners. But now—

Now, here we are, he thought. We know what to do and know how to do it!

Travis could hardly contain a smile as he glanced quickly at Laurie. She certainly wouldn't have to apologize to anyone for her appearance, at any rate! Her bright blue dress picked out the blue in her hazel eyes, and her long, wavy, auburn hair swung from Mother's tortoise-shell combs. Travis realized that she had taken pains to look as nice as possible. And her last minute inspection had made sure that Travis and Dana appeared at their best.

Wade interrupted his thoughts. "Laurie, Travis, Dana, this is your cousin, Kim."

The girl watched them without responding to their murmurs of greeting. Her solemn gaze passed quickly over Laurie and Travis to rest on Dana.

Wade looked at his daughter in amusement. "Dana's about your age, Kim. Let's see—Dana, you must be almost eight?"

"Yes, sir," Dana replied. She flipped one pigtail behind her shoulder and slid into a chair, giving Kim a tentative smile. Kim looked away. Travis waited, careful to seat his aunt first, then Laurie. He ignored Catherine's surprised glance and took the next seat.

Carefully, the children placed their napkins in their laps. A maid appeared immediately and served the meal. When she finished, Catherine picked up her fork.

The three McLarrens sat in awkward silence as the Shelvers began to eat. Dana glanced at her older sister and brother, toyed with her fork, then blurted, "Aren't we going to pray?"

Silverware clattered in the sudden silence. Wade glanced at Catherine's frown, then at Emily's barely suppressed grin.

He cleared his throat before saying, "Well, now, Dana, we—"

"Why don't you pray, Dana?" Emily asked the embarrassed girl.

Uncomfortably, Dana glanced at Laurie. Her sister nodded encouragingly. "Okay." Dana took a quick breath and began. "Dear God, thank you for the day that you gave us and that we got here safe. Help us to do what's right while we're here. Thank you for this food and please bless it, in Jesus' name. Amen."

Laurie's quiet "Amen" echoed her sister's. They looked up, once again, into a ring of faces. Travis's gaze moved around the table. Wade looked uncomfortable. Catherine's face was tight, her eyes downcast. Kim just looked back, her expression unreadable.

Wade glanced at his wife, and then turned to the children. "Well, I suppose you are eager to know more about what your situation here will be like."

No reply came, so he continued. "School will not open for two more weeks. When it does, Travis and Laurie will be attending Sweetoak Academy. Dana will go to Kim's school. Meanwhile, I will expect you to use these two weeks to accustom yourself to life here at Chellavue. You have access to any and all grounds here on the property, with the exception of the office wing out front. That is strictly off limits. Is that perfectly clear?"

Three heads nodded.

"Okay. Otherwise, roam around, find out what's here, use the stables, the pool, the recreation room if you like. Familiarize yourselves with Chellavue."

Travis put down his water glass. He hadn't been expecting a red carpet. However, Wade's next remark turned the excellent food bitter.

"When you begin school, I don't want you to display ignorance of your new home. If you have questions, ask. The servants, especially, are here for your convenience. I expect you to blend in here as properly as if you were my own children."

Travis saw two bright spots of red appear in Laurie's cheeks, but her voice answered with perfect control. "You are very thoughtful."

Outraged, Travis snapped, "We are not your children!"

"In your case," Wade said, "that is a little hard to forget. But you will be treated as Shelvers, out of respect to your mother." He threw his napkin down. "And the first step in that direction will be to supply you with a proper wardrobe. Emily, I imagine you would like to take care of that detail?"

His sister gave him an amused smile. "Yes, Wade, I would."

"We don't need anything." Travis protested.

"That will be for me to decide." Wade said the words flatly, regarding Travis with a cold look.

Laurie touched his arm, and Travis subsided. He concentrated on finishing his meal, but he was aware of the Shelvers, one by one, leaving the room until only Emily and the McLarrens remained.

"I want to go home," Dana said softly, almost in a whisper.

Even Laurie sat, head bent, pleating and unpleating her napkin. Travis felt that his heart had been wrenched out. "God," he said silently, "If You have such a perfect will in all this—well, it sure looks to me like You've messed up."

CHAPTER FIVE

SOME HORSE!

Travis awoke with a start. He lay still, trying to determine what had roused him from sleep. Then the sharp neigh of a horse came through the open balcony door. Travis flinched and turned his face to the wall. He studied the wood grain of the wall and tried to ignore the approaching hoof beats outside.

When he closed his eyes, his memory showed him a small black horse galloping across a rocky pasture. Travis threw the covers back with a swift jerk. Rolling out of bed, he hurried to the balcony. Down below, the big chestnut galloped over the rise. He charged toward the fence, pivoting at the last moment. Then he shook his head and looked toward the other horses that were being turned loose from the barn. With another exuberant neigh, the chestnut trotted off in their direction.

Travis watched until the horse disappeared into the hollow, then turned back to his room. He hated waking up this early with nothing to do. Five had been routine all of his life. But here, no one in the main house—not even the cooks—stirred before six or six-thirty. Most of the household didn't get up till closer to eight.

"These people come and go all hours of the night," Travis muttered, "then sleep half the morning away. When they do get together all they do is argue or party or watch television."

The last word brought a reluctant grin to his face. The first evening the whole family had gathered together in the den had been quite an experience. Evidently the program on the set was a favorite of the Shelvers. The McLarrens had never had a television set. In fact, Dana had rarely seen one.

Travis's grin grew broader as he remembered Dana's reaction to the plot.

"Why is the man with that lady?" she had asked with a puzzled frown.

"That's his girlfriend," Kim said importantly, sitting down beside Dana.

Startled, Dana stopped combing her doll's hair. "I thought he was married. You can't be married and have a girlfriend too!"

"Oh yes, you can."

"But that's wrong, isn't it—"

"No, no," Kim shook her shining hair. "You see, his wife is a real turkey, and—"

"That's not a very nice name to call somebody." Dana sat straight up in her chair.

"That's nothing. You ought to hear what they call her on the program! No wonder he found a girlfriend."

Dana looked at Wade thoughtfully. "Then does Uncle Wade have a girlfriend?"

Travis made no attempt to hide his grin as he watched his aunt's eyes grow fiery.

"Really, how naive!" Catherine stared at the child. "Haven't you ever seen a television? These people are just actors."

"Pretending?"

"Yes."

Dana hesitated. Then curiosity prodded her again. "Well, why do they pretend something that's wrong?"

At Catherine's sound of aggravation, Wade took over. "Maybe there are some people who choose to watch it, young lady. So why don't you be quiet so those of us who want to watch can do so?"

Travis stiffened as Dana's lips trembled. Silently, she picked up her doll and left the room. Before Travis could move, Kim had followed her. Scowling, he glanced at Laurie and got up. Laurie stood with him, asking to be excused. "Dana didn't mean to be rude," she said, "but Dad taught us not to fill our minds with thoughts and pictures that are wrong. If you'll excuse us?"

Emily caught Travis and Laurie in the hall and said quietly, "Let the girls go."

Laurie glanced after the departing figures of Kim and Dana. "Are you sure they'll be all right?"

Emily nodded. "Kim is a good child. She's left alone— well, her parents stay busy with work and charity affairs. Kim needs a friend, and I think Dana would be just the one for her. As a matter of fact, they will probably help each other."

Travis rolled over and sat up on the edge of the bed. Well, she was right, he thought.

Over the last few days, the girls had begun to spend more time together. And Laurie seemed to be gone most of the time, mostly shopping with Emily. That left Travis alone. Alone, and usually bored, just as he was this morning. I'll just check the stables, he thought. After all, we're supposed to *familiarize* ourselves with Chellavue!

That decision made, he stood up and went to the closet. Dressing was a ceremonial occasion these days. Emily had not scrimped on the shopping trips. All three McLarrens had been dragged around the entire Asheville shopping district. Now, their closets bulged. Travis surveyed the endless selection of pants and shirts. Then there were suits of every imaginable color—including three "good suits," as Emily called them. Now, he pushed past the new clothes and found one of the few pairs of jeans and a shirt he had been allowed to keep.

Ten minutes later, Travis strode confidently into the stable area. In the main barn, he found Ross Marlake, the head groom.

"I'd like to saddle a horse," Travis said firmly.

"So, you think you can ride?" The tall, weathered man stopped and looked Travis over.

Travis looked back. "Yes, sir. Your horses are different from ours, but I'd like to try them. I've ridden a lot."

"Well," Ross smiled, "out with it. Which one is it? One of them had to be special enough to make you break down and ask."

Travis felt his face grow warm, but didn't let his gaze waver. "The big chestnut that's always in the west pasture."

"Chellavue Flame! I might have known. Well, you do know a good horse when you see one, don't you?"

Travis shrugged. "Can I ride him, or not?"

"He's no cow pony, you know. And English riding is a lot different from Western style. Come on, let's see how you do."

Twenty minutes later Travis stood in the large exercise ring with one of the stable horses. Ross leaned on the fence, giving advice as it was needed. Before Travis mounted, he warned, "These horses are sensitive. You can control them by weight-shifting and the pressure of your legs. So don't haul around on their mouth like a rodeo buckaroo!"

Travis nodded, swinging up on the horse. He settled gently into the tiny English saddle, barely feeling the smooth leather beneath him. He bent his legs to fit into the short stirrups and gathered up the reins a little awkwardly. Grinning sheepishly, he looked down at Ross. "I feel like pushing my feet straight through the stirrups," he said.

Ross laughed. "You'll get used to it. Just relax."

Travis tightened his legs just a bit, and the horse stepped out in a purposeful walk. Travis adjusted himself to the motion of the horse, then touched his heels to the horse's sides. His mount stepped his pace up to a trot.

"You'll have to post," Ross said. "Move with the horse."

Accustomed to the short-stepping jog of Winsome, Travis found it difficult to catch the rhythm of the long, springing stride. Finally succeeding, he leaned forward, signaling the horse into an easy canter. Travis had a brief impression of quietly flowing water before he snapped his attention back to the business at hand.

"Good! Now take him into a canter," Ross ordered.

Bracing himself, Travis tightened his right leg against the horse's side, and leaned slightly to the left. That would have been enough to make Winsome spin instantly on her hindquarters. This horse's response was just as quick, but it was as smooth as well-oiled machinery. Travis swung to the left, as though following an orbital pattern, and cut directly across the ring.

"Don't pull up! Bend your wrists down a little."

Travis obeyed, and the next two strides brought the horse to an even halt. Travis grinned. Leaning right and bringing his left heel in quickly, he sent the horse in a cantering circle to the right. Coming back to the top of the circle, Travis touched the horse's side with his right heel. There was an almost imperceptible shift in stride as the horse changed leads and swung into a figure eight.

Twenty minutes later, Travis felt himself growing tired. Trying to remember Ross's quick commands and retain control of the horse taxed his strength. The horse moved as smoothly as ever, with only the smallest spots of dampness on his coat.

"Maybe I underestimated you. You've seen a horse more than once or twice, haven't you?" Ross's darkly tanned face spread into a wide grin. "I'll make a deal with you. If you'll do a few more practice sessions here with me, I'll find a horse for you. Won't be Flame—not for a while yet, if ever. He's Mrs. Shelver's horse."

"Really?" Travis couldn't hide his surprise. "She rides?"

"Sure," the groom snapped a lead rein on the horse. "Used to show the horses all the time. She competed against Emily years ago in the show at Huntington. That's how she met your uncle. All the Shelvers were there."

Travis walked beside him as he led the horse back to the stable. "I haven't seen her riding."

"Doesn't do too much, lately. She's tied up with that new hospital project in town. Raising money."

"Then how does Flame get his exercise?"

"In the field. And I ride him some to keep him trained properly." The groom looked at Travis keenly. "Better stay off that horse, son. You don't know enough about his training to ride him. Not yet, anyway."

Travis shrugged. Turning back to the horse, he began to remove the saddle.

Ross was quiet for a moment, then spoke again. "There's quite a few really good horses around here. I'm a bit picky about who I let ride. But I sure could use some help. Sometimes it's hard to find enough time to exercise all the horses properly."

"Why do they keep so many horses?" Travis almost interrupted. "There must be at least twenty."

"Twenty-six, counting the ponies and the weanlings." Ross raised a questioning eyebrow at Travis, but kept his tone steady. "Habit, more than anything else, probably. There have always been horses at Chellavue and probably always will be. They make good entertainment for guests, and pleasant pastime for the family. Then, again, when the horses are shown, they always place well."

"Anybody else show besides Mrs. Shelver?"

"Everybody, at one time or the other, except Mr. Shelver. He doesn't care much for riding. He likes to see them shown, though."

"Hmm." Travis patted the horse's shoulder. "Can I put him up?"

"Sure." Ross stepped back out of the way as Travis led the horse toward the barn door. "His tack goes on the last hanger on the right in the tack room."

It didn't take Travis more than fifteen minutes to take care of the horse and leave him comfortable in his stall. Then he lingered on in the stable, taking his time inhaling the familiar smells of leather and hay. He wandered up and down the aisles of stalls, patting noses and distributing carrots he got from Ross.

Travis felt his frustrations ease for the first time in days. The people who own the horses might be hard and strange, and the horses might look a little different, but animals are the same the world over, he concluded.

He stopped one last time at Flame's stall and gave the big chestnut the last carrot. "You're some horse," he said softly, rubbing Flame's nose. "I sure like you better than I like the people here."

CHAPTER SIX

SWEETOAK ACADEMY

Emily Shelver seemed to delight in doting on the McLarrens, including Travis. This morning, when Travis reached the breakfast table, he found a steaming-hot loaf of banana bread near his plate. In the past banana bread had been a rare treat for him, a treat from his mother's oven. Now that his Aunt Emily knew he liked it, he found it served frequently.

Unfortunately, however, Emily was nowhere in sight this morning, and Aunt Catherine dominated the breakfast table. She fussed at the maid and questioned everyone about school preparations until Travis was ready to scream.

"Now, Kim, you make sure you don't have Miss Dunham for your homeroom teacher. If they give you any trouble, you call me and I'll talk to them. Laurie, are you quite sure you remember who Mr. McGuire is?"

"Yes, ma'am." Laurie took the last bite of her bacon.

"Remember that both of you will need to see him as soon as you get there. The third door on the left."

"I remember," Laurie assured her calmly. Travis looked at his sister. She was poised and smiling, dressed in a grey and yellow plaid jumper. Travis was pleased to note that, although the clothes were obviously new and well-cut, she wore their mother's locket nestled at her throat.

"Well, then," Catherine sighed, "are all of you ready? I don't want any last-minute slapdashery on the opening day of school. And Laurie, drive carefully."

"Of course!" Laurie rose, smiling. "Hey, guys—are you ready to go?" Travis caught a note of eagerness in her voice.

"Yeah, sure," he said, glancing sideways at her as he left his chair. Dana and Kim followed as they went to the hall to collect their things.

"Remember," Catherine called after them as they went out the door, "when you see—"

Travis groaned and let the door swing shut. "Honestly!"

Later, Travis remembered that day for its frantic pace. They went from place to place, office to office, from registration to class, and from class to meetings. He gave and signed his name a hundred times. He actually grew used to answering, "I live with Wade Shelver. No, he's my uncle."

Travis was mildly astonished at the effect the Shelver name seemed to have on people. "Hey, Red!" several boys called out to him as he stood by his locker between classes. One came up and jostled Travis with his elbow. "You're new here, aren't you?" At Travis's nod, he continued. "Well, you have to come over here and tell us a little about yourself. We want to know what's walking around our halls." The others laughed appreciatively.

"What's your name, Red?" someone called.

Travis didn't go any nearer to them, but turned around and said, "I'm Travis McLarren. Who are you?"

"I'm Gary, and that's Mike and Rob and Scott. Think you can keep that straight?"

Travis leaned back against his locker and hooked his thumbs in his belt loops. For a supposedly high-class school, he thought, they sure are rude.

"Where are you from, anyway?" Gary demanded.

"Well," Travis said, raising an eyebrow, "I'm from here, now. I moved here from Kentucky a couple weeks ago."

"Kentucky hillbilly, huh?"

Travis smiled as he glanced down at the clothing he wore. He knew he didn't look like a hillbilly. "Call it what you like. I don't answer to you." He turned to his locker to collect his books.

"If you don't think you're a hillbilly, Red, then what's your dad do?"

"Not much," he said shortly. "My parents were killed a month ago. That's why I'm here now."

"Oh, yeah?" The one called Rob spoke up. "Where are you staying?"

"Chellavue."

A moment of silence greeted that statement. "Why's that?" There seemed to be some hesitation in Rob's voice.

"Wade Shelver's my uncle. My mother grew up there."

"Oh," Rob started to backtrack, "well, we weren't trying to give you a hard time or anything—"

"We weren't?" Gary cut in, taking a step toward Travis. "So I suppose you think you're some kind of a hot-shot now, huh?" Gary grabbed Travis's arm roughly and pulled him forward. "Let me tell you something about—"

Travis seized Gary's jacket with his free hand and gave a twisting jerk and a shove, as though he were throwing a calf. Gary slammed into the metal lockers with a resounding crash. Recovering quickly, the older boy spun toward Travis, but a man's voice interrupted them.

"Boys! What's going on down there?"

Travis ignored the man. Keeping his attention on Gary, he narrowed his eyes. "Let me tell you something, whatever-your-name-was, you'll find out that I don't like it when people try to push me around!"

Travis slammed his locker door in disgust and walked away. Clattering down the front steps of the school, he looked around for Laurie. She wasn't difficult to spot.

Laurie was leaning against a tall flower planter. A young man and a slender girl stood beside her. Travis couldn't hear what they were saying, but as he came close, he could hear the end of Laurie's answer. "It sounds great. You don't know how much I've missed our church back home. I'll call and let you know."

"Okay. See you later, Laurie," the girl said. The two disappeared into the stream of students headed for the buses and the parking lot.

"Who's that?" Travis asked.

"Renee and Brad. They asked us to attend their church. You know, the little one on the way to Chellavue."

"Oh." Travis rested against the planter. "This school is a real zero."

"It's different, all right," Laurie agreed. "But I did meet some nice people. I really like Renee. And she lives just down the road from us."

"You're ahead of me," Travis grumbled. "I'd like to know how you always seem to meet people you like and I run into the losers."

Laurie opened her mouth as if to answer, then closed it. Without speaking, they drove to the elementary school to pick up Dana and Kim. Then they drove back to Chellavue.

Upon arrival, all three McLarrens went upstairs to shed their school clothes. Laurie announced her intentions to help her aunt on a project. Travis knew that Dana would soon be in the library, nose buried in her latest book. Travis opened his balcony doors and changed to his jeans.

If the word *farm* hadn't jumped out at him Travis might not have even paid attention to the voices. As it was, he stopped abruptly and stood listening, shirt half buttoned.

"What kind of yield do you expect on the money from the farm?"

Wade's voice answered. "Not much, with interest rates the way they are."

Travis moved quietly out onto the balcony. Listening carefully, he identified the other voice as belonging to the lawyer that had visited the farm.

"Then I suggest investing the money." The persistent attorney went on. "You have the authority to decide where to keep it. Or what to do with it."

"So you say," Wade said dryly.

"Okay, then. We put it in stocks. The kids will never know the difference in the amount that it makes in the next few years."

"All right. We'll try it your way." The voices were fading. Travis felt his face grow red-hot.

"You cheat! Fake! User!" The words tumbled out in a hoarse whisper. "I was right!" Travis took the stairs several at a time. Running down the hall, he slammed the door behind him. "You're going to make a neat profit from our farm, Uncle!"

Travis ripped a branch from a shrub as he walked by. Tearing the leaves from it, he broke the branch into tiny pieces and flung it away. "I won't make it easy for you, that's for sure!"

CHAPTER SEVEN
JUST ENDURING

Travis developed a regular habit of going to the stables immediately after school. He headed first to Flame's stall, always with some treat tucked into his pocket for the big horse. Though he groomed the other horses meticulously, he lingered over Flame's red coat. The first time the horse whinnied as Travis came in marked a red-letter day for the boy.

Ross and the other grooms became accustomed to Travis's afternoon visits. But when Ross arrived at the stables Saturday morning and found Travis waiting, even he was surprised.

"What in the world are you doing here?" Ross scratched his head. "Do you know what time it is?"

"Yes. Five-thirty." Travis made a wry face. "If you don't need me here, I can always go sit in my room and wait for everyone else to wake up."

Ross stared at him for a moment, and then his tanned face split into his usual wide grin. "Hmph!" he laughed. "Can't break old habits, hmm?"

"I guess not." Travis followed him into the barn. "At home, I had chores to do before school. I had to get up early."

"So, how's it going up at the big house?"

"I hate it up there!" Travis's temper flashed out briefly. 'I'd rather be here. I like it here."

Ross frowned and looked Travis directly in the eye. "Well, there's plenty to do here. I think it's about time you told your uncle what you're doing, though. I'm not in the habit of keeping things from my boss."

"I don't really care." Travis shrugged. "He's told me I can do as I like."

Ross shook his head. "All right, then, come on."

Travis spent the morning mucking out the stables along with the grooms. Then he dragged hay bales from the loft and dropped them to the barn floor. He unfastened the hay and loaded loose hay into a wheelbarrow. Trundling the barrow to the stables, he forked loose hay into the stalls. By the time Ross called a halt for lunch, he was hot, tired and dirty.

He looked at his watch and glanced down at his clothes. "Uh, oh," he said, letting out his breath in a soft whistle, "I've got two choices. Late for lunch or dirty for lunch."

Common sense warned him that the first evil would be far better than the second. He put the equipment away quickly and headed for the back of Chellavue, hoping to slip through the kitchen and up the back stairs. Unfortunately, Catherine was in the kitchen dealing with a distraught cook.

"Well, *don't* hold the meal any longer. If he's late, he'll just have to do with—" Catherine's eyes widened as she took in Travis's appearance.

"What on earth have you been doing?" she asked furiously. "Just look at you—and we have guests for lunch!"

Travis cringed inwardly as the icy blue eyes stabbed at him, but he forced his face to go blank. "Working," he said impulsively. "Good *honest* work, which is more than I can say of some people around here!"

Catherine's face paled. "Go to your room and stay there! Your uncle will speak to you after our guests are gone!"

Sullenly, Travis stomped up the stairs. When he reached his room, he flung himself onto his bed without removing his stained clothing. Reaching over, he flipped on the radio and turned up the volume. Then he put his arm over his eyes to shut out the room.

When Laurie knocked on the door, he had fallen asleep. He rolled over and, burying his face in the bedspread, called in a muffled voice, "Come on in."

He didn't look up until Laurie touched his shoulder. She started at the wild glare in his eyes.

"Travis!"

"Sorry," he mumbled. "I thought it was him."

"You mean Uncle Wade?"

"I mean *Wade*." Travis frowned.

"Travis, why are you behaving like this?" Laurie asked gently. "Sure, I know Uncle Wade and Aunt Catherine might not be the easiest people to know, but we have to try. After all, we are the strangers in their house, not the other way around. They didn't have to take us in, you know."

"I sure wish they hadn't!" His gaze flicked over her silky dress. "But I can't expect you to agree. Mom and Dad could never have given you all the loot you've collected lately!"

"Travis!"

His gaze wavered, then dropped. "I'm sorry, Laurie."

He sat up slowly and rubbed his face with his hands. "It's just that nothing goes right for me. I don't belong here, Laurie."

"Of course you do," Laurie looked shocked. "You are one of us, one of the family."

"I'm not so sure any more." Travis shook his head. "You and Dana, maybe, but not me. You seem to fit in fine, Laurie. And Dana seems happy enough with Kim and Aunt Emily, but me? I hardly even see you two any more!"

"That's not by our choice, Travis," Laurie said, gently pushing the hair out of his eyes. "You're just not around much."

"I stay out of *their* way as much as possible," Travis responded, bitterness returning.

"But by avoiding the Shelvers, you aren't accomplishing anything. Remember, Dad always taught us to face our problems and try to work them out? During devotions this morning, I read the passage he liked so much—"

Travis knew the verse. He cut her off quickly.

"But you don't know what I heard!" He leaned forward tensely. "Wade is planning to invest our money and use the interest himself. I heard him talking with that lawyer of his. I told you he was a cheat!"

"Travis, listen!" Tears glistened in Laurie's eyes. "Can't you see that what he has spent on us already is more than he could ever gain from what we had? He's helping us, not hurting us!"

"And you're deaf, dumb, and blind! I don't want charity! I want what's legally mine!"

Laurie shook her head. "Travis, let's pray about it together. God can take care of this whole mess. You know He can!"

"You can pray if you want to! I'm going to do something about it!"

Travis swung himself off the bed and charged through the bedroom door. He met his uncle coming up the stairs. Without speaking, he brushed past the startled man and rushed down the stairs.

"Travis!"

The door cut off whatever Wade Shelver had intended to say. For a moment he stared at Laurie, who had come down the hall. Then he turned and, shoulders slumped, went back the same direction he had come.

CHAPTER EIGHT
A VISIT TO THE PAST

Driving rain beat against the windows of the Chellavue manor. Inside the glass doors of his balcony, Travis watched the tree-tops dip and sway in the wind. A frown creased his face as he remembered the speech Wade had finally delivered in the study downstairs. "Shape up or get out," was Travis's version of it, though Wade had put things a little more diplomatically. If it hadn't been for Dana and Laurie, he would have packed and left for the mountains that night. But to leave them alone, here in this house—he couldn't do it.

The rain drummed in tempo with his thoughts. Travis paced around his room for a few moments, then stepped out into the hall. He passed Laurie's room. The door was open, and Laurie's head was bent over a large book. Travis recognized his father's Bible and walked quickly on. Down the hall, he stopped at Dana's room. Tapping softly on the door, Travis was careful not to raise his voice as he called, "Hey, Dana?"

Dana did not respond, so Travis pushed the door open slightly. Dana was sprawled on the bed, fast asleep, her latest book still open beside her. "Great," Travis's voice dropped to a mutter again. He pulled the door shut and started downstairs. "Back to the library, I guess."

Travis wasn't sure why he felt he had to be so quiet, except that the emptiness of the enormous house seemed to forbid noise of any sort. The steady ticking of the giant grandfather clock at the foot of the stairs sounded abnormally loud.

Wade and Catherine Shelver had been out of town for a few days, and Travis had not seen anyone else since breakfast. Since he had been forbidden to go to the stables until the Shelvers returned, Travis had nothing to do. He almost wished it were a school day, so that he would have something to occupy his mind.

He wandered down the long, broad hallway, glancing into the rooms on his right as he went. This branch of his uncle's home never failed to amaze him. It contained not only the library and a music room but also two complete guest suites—complete apartments within themselves.

He stopped in the doorway to the living room of the larger suite. Shaking his head, he grinned in wry amusement. The entire room was furnished, carpeted, and draped in deep shades of turquoise and cream. A white marble fireplace stood at one end of the room, and an antique roll-top desk at the other. Several doors opened from the living room. Travis knew that they led to a kitchen alcove, two bedrooms, a full bath, and an entrance to the outside patio.

Travis chuckled softly as he realized that in the last few months the suite had been occupied only twice—and then only for a day or two. "Not in our wildest dreams!" he said aloud. "I wonder if Dad ever had a chance to see all this?"

Travis left the guest room and continued toward the library. A rainy, boring Saturday was a perfect time to browse for some new books. The Shelvers' library had plenty of room for browsing, too. The room was enormous, like everything else in the house. The wall at the far end boasted a miniature gallery of huge paintings. Bookshelves covered the other walls from floor to ceiling. Classics, adventure, romance, history, encyclopedias, atlases, fiction, biographies—Travis knew that the quantity of books here would embarrass the public library in his small mountain town.

Turning toward a section he had not yet explored, Travis began inspecting the book jackets. Absently he wandered toward the far corner of the room and found himself amidst beautiful geographical picture books. A book on a high shelf with the words *Northern Appalachians* on its cover caught his eye. He pulled over one of the several stepladders in the room and set out after the big blue volume.

Not until he was level with the top shelf did Travis see the picture albums. They had been shoved carelessly on their sides, as far back toward the wall as they would go. Travis frowned in curiosity as he picked one up and flipped it open. Almost instantly the frown vanished. Less than a minute later, Travis was seated on the floor with the picture albums strewn about him, the first one opened in his lap.

Travis was so engrossed in the album that he didn't hear the library door open. Kim entered the room, stopping short at the sight of her cousin.

"Oh, I thought you were Dana." She took a step backwards, as if to leave, then squinted her eyes at the albums he held.

"Travis!" she squealed. He looked up, startled. "Where did you find those?" Kim almost ran across the room toward him.

"Up on one of the shelves. Why? What's it matter to you?"

"Those are the old albums with all your mother's pictures, aren't they?" Kim reached for one, and Travis couldn't think fast enough to stop her. "I've wanted to see the rest of these for so long, but I didn't know where they were—I mean, they've got pictures of my mom and dad, too, you know, and everybody else. But Daddy found me looking at them one day a long time ago, and he got really upset and took them. I haven't seem them since."

Travis looked at her, puzzled. "Why?"

"Oh, you know. Daddy always gets mad whenever anybody talks about your parents."

"I know that. I mean, why does he get so mad? Nobody has ever bothered to explain."

"Well, I'm not real sure—oh, Travis, please let me see that one!" She reached for the book, but Travis held it back.

"Only if you'll tell me what you know about them."

"Okay! I promise. Just give me that—" Kim wrestled the album away from Travis. Opening it up, she started flipping through the pages. "Oh, here we go. This is where I left off." Kim sighed in satisfaction and began pointing out people and places.

"See here, this is your mother, and Aunt Emily, and Daddy. This is the house out at the shore. We still go there for awhile every summer. But I guess Daddy was only about seventeen then, and Aunt Grace and Aunt Emily were younger."

Travis looked closely at the picture. Three young people sat on the steps of a large cabin. All three wore big smiles, and their dark hair blew about their faces. Travis could barely tell which girl was his mother and which one was his Aunt Emily.

"Boy, they sure did look alike," Kim commented. Travis started, thinking for a moment that he had spoken his thoughts aloud. But Kim didn't notice. "Aunt Emily says that they all used to be really good friends. Not like now."

"What happened?" Travis demanded. "Mom and Dad would never really talk about it. I mean, I have sort of an idea, but—"

"Hey, you two." Dana spoke from the doorway. She stood, still rumpled from sleep, holding her book. "What's going on?"

"Come on in, Dana," Travis said. "Take a look at these pictures."

He and Kim moved over to let Dana look.

"Dana," Kim said with a thoughtful look on her face, "did you really like it way up there in those mountains? I mean, everything is so much nicer here—"

"Yeah!" Travis interrupted, glaring at her. "She 'really did like it.' And what would you know about what it's like up there?"

Kim ignored the question. "I guess I know you did. You and Laurie and Dana always get along so good. I just wondered why that was—and what your parents were really like."

"My parents are none of your business!" Travis replied. "I know what you and your whole family think—"

"Well, if you can ask questions, so can I!" Kim shot back.

"I guess I have a right to ask!" Travis's temper exploded. He jerked the album out of Kim's hands. "Look at that! That's all I have left of my mom! You've still got your folks! I think I ought to be able to ask a few questions about why everybody hated my parents!"

"Stop it, both of you!" Dana looked from one to the other.

Kim ignored her and glared straight back at Travis in defiance. Stubbornly, the two remained in a stare-down until another soft voice spoke.

"Do you really want to know, Travis?" Both Kim and Travis jumped. They all turned to face Emily Shelver, who had entered the library unheard, during the heat of their quarrel.

"Yes." Travis got to his feet and handed Dana the album. "Yes. I want to know. I've never seen such a bunch of back-stabbing people in my whole life—I've got to live here, and I don't even know why everybody hates each other."

Emily laughed softly. "We don't hate each other, really, Travis. And you're not usually very 'loving' yourself, you know." Seating herself on a footstool, Emily picked up one of the albums. "Come back over here, Travis, and sit down. Let me tell you a story that started, oh, I guess it was about six years before you were even born."

Driven by his curiosity, Travis pulled up another footstool near to his aunt's side. She opened the album to a page near the front. "These were my parents. Your grandparents. I guess the whole thing started when my father died of a heart attack. I was just your age, Travis, fourteen. Grace was eighteen, and Wade, twenty-four. He was old enough to inherit control of Chellavue, of the family, and of all Dad's businesses. He took his responsibilities seriously, maybe too seriously.

"Of course, Father's death was hard on all of us, but I think Grace suffered the most. She had been very close to Father, and his death was completely unexpected. Not

long after the funeral, she visited a little church not far from here."

"Our church?" Dana asked in surprise.

"Yes, it's the same one that you and Laurie have been going to. But your mother just wandered into it one day. She told me later that she had been looking for something— just what, she wasn't sure—but she found *it* there. Grace talked a lot about having been *saved* and how happy she was. I guess I really didn't listen to her very much then. I was just glad that she had stopped moping around so much. We'd been worried about her.

"Anyway, Wade never approved of Grace's going to church, but he never really forbade her to go. She continued to attend there a lot for about a year. Then one day, guess what happened?" Emily flipped a page and pointed to a picture of Grace Shelver and two tall red-headed men.

"Dad!" Dana said, leaning forward to look.

"And Uncle James!" Travis added.

"Yes. Your father and his brother stopped at the church, because they knew the pastor. When Travis met Grace, he stayed on a while, and James returned to the farm alone. He came back for the wedding, though."

"Uncle James," Travis supplied. "I remember him and Aunt Beth. She used to bring me toy soldiers. She and Uncle James never had children of their own. But when he was killed in Vietnam, she went back to live near her parents."

"Um-hmm." Emily nodded. "We heard that he had been reported missing in action in Saigon just a few months before the American troops were withdrawn. You must have been about eleven?"

"Yes," Travis replied, thinking for a moment, "but I hadn't seen him for four years."

Emily paused for a long moment. Then Travis interrupted the silence. "Uncle Wade didn't like my dad, did he?"

"Try to understand, Travis, how different your father was from anything we had ever known. He was unbelievably sold out on this religion that Grace had just picked up. Wade just could not stand that. Plus, Wade had set his heart on seeing Grace marry a friend of his. Grace, of course, said that she could never even consider it, because the man was not a *Christian*.

"I'm sure you can imagine that, as stubborn as Wade is, and as much as Grace was in love, this soon developed into an all-out war. Ultimately, Grace said she would marry Travis, your father, because she 'knew it was God's will' for her. Wade said she would not, because, as head of the family, he absolutely forbade it. If she did so, he said she would be leaving this house forever. He thought that would stop her."

"But she went!" Travis said aloud, thinking that he would have gone too.

"Yes, but it cost her a lot to do so," Emily continued. "Mother died shortly after the wedding. Wade blamed it on the stress Grace had caused, and he never forgave her for that."

Emily closed the photo album and folded her hands on top of it. "He told Grace that she was disowned and was never to set foot on Chellavue again."

Travis's face darkened. "It wasn't her fault!"

"No, Travis, it wasn't, really. It wasn't anyone's fault. But Wade didn't see it that way. Neither did I at the time. Nor did your mother." Emily bit her lip and paused before continuing. "Just as Grace had been close to Dad, I was close to Mother. Her death upset me so that I'm afraid I wasn't much help to Grace. Anyway, she and your dad moved to Kentucky, and that's the last time any of us ever saw her. Oh, she wrote sometimes. And sometimes she called and I talked to her. Of course Wade wouldn't. It was too late as far as he was concerned. He would never let himself back down from a decision he had made—even though I think he wanted to."

Emily stood up and began stacking the photo albums back on the shelf. "Wade always looked upon the whole incident as a black mark on the family. But as the years went by, his love for his sister won out, in a way. And eventually he convinced himself that it was all your father's fault—I know!" Emily waved aside Travis's objection. "I know it wasn't. But once upon a time, this family was very close. Wade missed his sister terribly. He was very upset at the losses in the family, and it's human nature to blame everything you dislike on someone else—you do that yourself sometimes, Travis."

"Well, why can't this mess get straightened out?" Dana asked bluntly.

Emily sat down again, a thoughtful look coming to her face. "I used to ask your mother that when she called. She always said that she was willing to put the whole thing behind her, but she knew Wade probably never would, unless he became a Christian. She said she knew that only God could straighten out the mess we'd made of our family."

Emily sighed. "I always thought that what she said made no sense—until I met her children. You all are different, you know. Your sisters even more so than you, Travis. And Laurie is so much like what your mother was at that age—but yet so content, in spite of everything." Emily paused for a long moment. "I'll tell you that it's enough to make me wonder if there was something to what Grace said."

Kim spoke up again. "Dana tells me all about God. Travis, do you believe in God too?"

"I don't think so. I used to think I did, but I don't see how God, if He's supposed to care about us so much, could let things happen like they have."

"You don't think that maybe things can work out in some way?" Emily asked softly. "Maybe some good can come of this."

"Well, I tell you one thing that won't work out. Uncle Wade cheated us out of our farm. It's sold and gone now. There won't be any working that out!"

"My daddy didn't cheat!" Kim flashed.

"Ha! That shows what you know about it!"

"Hey, you two! Don't start this again—"

"Don't you start defending him!" Travis interrupted his aunt. "You know I'm right!"

"Travis, you have to learn to live with and work with things that you can't do anything about! You can't change what's done, so why don't you—"

"I guess I should have known!" Travis glared at his aunt. "The whole story was just a lead-up to another sermon. But I'll tell you that I hate it here, and I never asked to come here! And that thief is never going to walk on me!"

"He's not a thief!" Kim started to cry.

"Travis!" Dana put her arms around Kim.

"Travis, I think that's enough." Emily looked at Travis firmly.

"You better believe it's enough. Enough of a lot of things. At least now I know more about what he's like. I guess I should thank you for the information." Travis gave a mock salute and walked out of the library.

CHAPTER NINE
JUST LIKE DAD SAID

After his uncle returned, he and Catherine gave Travis permission to work with the horses, provided he stayed away from Flame, Catherine's horse. Travis agreed, willing to do anything to work with the horses. Except for the horses, Travis didn't really look forward to anything. He spent more and more of his time at the stables, and withdrew more and more from the Shelver household.

The weeks rolled into months. September, October, November . . . still the weather stayed warm. Travis, used to snowy mountain winters, found this just another part of his boredom and disgust with the never-ending routine he lived.

One day in mid-November, Travis was sitting at his desk in school. He had finished his history test early and sat slumped in his seat, glancing around at the other students. He hadn't really had much trouble becoming accepted by his classmates, but neither had he made any effort to be friends with any of them. Most of them he distrusted, thinking that they would want to gloat over being friends with someone from Chellavue.

Travis's wandering eye stopped on a boy on the far side of the room: Brad Koppell, the brother of Laurie's friend, Renee. This church business is getting out of hand, really, Travis thought. I bet Uncle Wade would stop that pretty fast, if he kept any better track of us. They're always down there now. Travis had to smile at the thought of Chellavue being regularly represented in a little wooden-frame Baptist church. It wasn't quite the image that the Shelvers tried for.

The bell jolted him out of his reverie. Travis gathered up his things, deposited his test on the teacher's desk, and left the room.

"Hey, Travis, how did it go?" Travis turned around to see Brad beside him.

"Not too bad, really. Could have been a lot worse."

"Mr. Brain strikes again!" Brad's friendly grin made the comment a joke. "Travis, how am I ever going to be able to talk you into coming to church with us?"

"You probably won't," Travis said. "You've asked a dozen times now. I've told you I don't want to go. No one can make me, either."

"I guess not." Brad's voice was calm. "You know, as much as Laurie says you don't get along with Shelvers, I think you're starting to fit in there pretty well."

Travis stopped in the middle of the bustling hall. "Why do you say that?" His eyes narrowed.

"Because you walk around here in your own world, doing exactly what you want to do, carrying a fifty-pound chip on your shoulder." Brad met Travis's angry glare without flinching. "No one 'makes' Wade Shelver do anything either."

Travis turned and walked on, intending to leave Brad behind, but the other boy came right behind him. "Travis

McLarren, don't you have any respect for what your parents tried to teach you about God?"

"Back off, Koppell. You don't know anything about my parents."

"I know your sisters, and I've found out what they knew before they came here. Don't try to tell me that you don't at least know about the same things. In fact," Brad continued doggedly, "I bet you know you're wrong in not going. That's why you won't go. You couldn't last through a single service without admitting it."

Travis stopped at his locker. "I'll admit one thing: you're a pain in the neck. What would it prove to you if I went?"

"That you're not scared, and that you don't already know you're wrong."

Travis dumped his books in a careless heap. "Okay, when do I go?"

"There's a special service tonight."

"Fine. When?"

"Around seven-thirty. Laurie and Dana are coming. You can ride with them."

The church's small interior was furnished completely in light-colored woodwork. Many people came over to greet him as he sat with his sisters and the Koppell family. The pastor, John Riordan, was especially friendly. "Well, well," he said, shaking Travis's hand briskly. "You're the other McLarren, that's easy to see—the spitting image of your dad, Travis." The elderly man smiled. "It's good to have you with us."

"Thanks." Travis didn't feel like extending the conversation. The service began shortly. Travis could hardly believe the enthusiasm with which the people sang. The songs were familiar, though. They brought back memories of a rustic old church set up on a rocky hillside of a mountain.

Travis shut out that memory as quickly as possible and set out to block the speaker from his thoughts as well. The preacher was a grizzled, white-haired old man whom Pastor Riordan had introduced as a visiting evangelist. Travis soon discovered, however, that this little old man could not be ignored for long. In spite of himself, Travis became aware of the verses that the preacher read from the Bible.

" 'For God sent not His Son into the world to condemn the world; but that the world through Him might be saved. He that believeth on him is not condemned; but he that believeth not is condemned already, because he hath not believed in the name of the only begotten Son of God. . . . For every one that doeth evil hateth the light, neither cometh to the light, lest his deeds should be reproved.' "

"I bet you know you're wrong." Brad's words echoed in Travis's mind.

"Jesus Christ says, 'I am the way, the truth, and the life. . . .' " The preacher went on, but Travis's memory played tricks on him. As he heard the words from the Bible, the rows of pews before his eyes vanished. Once again he was high up in the Smoky Mountains, trotting along the Stone Ridge trail on Winsome. His father rode beside Travis, his rich baritone voice resounding from the hillsides.

To God be the glory, great things He hath done!
So loved He the world that He gave us His Son.
Who yielded His life an atonement for sin,
And opened the life-gate that all may go in!

Travis tried to concentrate on the sunset outside the church, but the old preacher's words pushed into his thoughts with insistence. "You can spend your whole life fighting it. Some of you may have heard about Christ since the day you were born, but you sit here tonight and refuse to accept what He did for you." The little man's face flushed, and his voice rose. "Well, let me tell you something, my friend. God has the power and the right to judge sin—and He will! And the sin that will send you to hell is the sin of rejecting Christ!"

The church faded out again. This time Travis sprawled on the floor in front of the fireplace in the McLarren's old mountain home. The whole family gathered there after supper. Travis remembered the way the firelight flickered and reflected from the black cover of the Bible from which his father read.

" 'He that believeth on the Son hath everlasting life, and he that believeth not on the Son shall not see life, but the wrath of God abideth on him.' " His father looked up. "We need to recognize the importance of this. Almost every day," the words marched out of forgotten corners in Travis's memory, "you kids have contact with people who have never acknowledged Jesus Christ as their Lord."

He glanced at his wife, and Travis thought of the many times she had requested prayer for her own family in Asheville. Then he continued, "As you meet people, I hope your testimony is clear. Hell is an actual place, just as that fire there is real. It's our responsibility to spread the gospel so that people can know there is a way to escape it."

Travis began to wish for the service to end. The preacher went on and on, reading old, familiar verses, and telling the same, familiar story. But something new stirred in Travis tonight. Everything the little old man said resurrected a memory of his parents' faith. A restlessness—a discomfort—forced Travis to fight to control his fidgeting.

The preacher's voice continued, salt in the sore of Travis's uneasiness. "God wants everyone to come to Him.

He has a special plan for each of your lives, but you must choose to let Him work."

Travis picked up a hymnal and gripped it with sweaty hands. Why? his thoughts demanded. Why does it never work for me, when it was so real to them?

"All you have to do is ask Him to save you. 'The Lord is nigh unto all them that call upon Him.' "

Travis's heart began beating faster as another memory crowded into his mind. He crouched with his sisters in the small cellar under their kitchen. Lightning and hail crashed about the house, and deafening thunder shook the ground, almost drowning out the distant roar of the tornado. Dana screamed, "Mommy, Mommy!" over and over, as Laurie desperately tried to calm her. Travis remembered his frantic prayer.

"God, protect my parents! Mom and Dad are out there; God, please help them!"

Travis's jaw clenched. He bent the cover of the hymnbook so tightly that it began to burst its binding. God, where were You then? he asked silently. The ceiling of that basement was like galvanized steel! I couldn't get through it to You! What happened to Your "special plan" for my parents' lives? They're dead now! You wouldn't save them, You wouldn't let us stay on the farm, and now we have to live with cheating, back-stabbing people. How am I supposed to "accept Your will"? How can You love us and allow these things to happen?

Travis could barely contain his tears as the congregation rose to sing.

> My soul in sad exile was out on life's sea,
> So burdened with sin and distress.
> Till I heard a sweet voice, saying "Make me your choice,"
> And I entered the haven of rest.

"Give in to God," the preacher pleaded in a near whisper. His voice was a magnet that seemed to pull with a nearly physical force. "Stop fighting, and let Him take charge. God alone has the answers to your problems." Travis thought he was going to be sick to his stomach.

I've anchored my soul in the haven of rest
I'll sail the wide seas no more.
The tempest may sweep o'er the wide stormy deep,
But in Jesus, I'm safe ever more. . . .

At last it ended. Travis turned to Brad. "Are you happy now?" Travis was surprised his voice could still sound so calm when his insides churned so badly.

"I'm glad you came, Travis," Brad said, stepping out into the aisle and letting Laurie pass. "We hope to see you here again."

Travis didn't answer. He followed Dana, then turned, and went out. He spent the next fifteen minutes slumped in the car, waiting for the girls.

CHAPTER TEN
FRUSTRATION

"Morning, Travis!"

Kim and Dana climbed up on the fence rail by Travis.

"He's beautiful, isn't he, Travis?" Dana asked, watching Flame gallop across the field. "He moves so lightly. Riding him would be like riding a cloud."

"He's big, though," Kim said. "Big and strong. I wouldn't want to ride him, but you ought to see Mother handle him!"

Travis frowned. "I bet I wouldn't have any trouble with him. He likes me, see?"

He pulled a carrot from his shirt and held it out, calling softly. The big chestnut swung around and stood, head held high, listening.

"Come on, Flame. Come on," Travis coaxed.

Flame tossed his head and, whinnying softly, trotted toward the boy.

"See," Travis said, rubbing the horse's nose, "We get along just fine."

Kim grinned, blowing a strand of straight hair out of her face. "Better not try riding him, though. Mother would be furious!"

She slid down from the rail. "Come on, Dana."

Dana jumped down, then stopped to look back at Travis. "Kim's going to teach me to ride English style. Come watch, Travis, please."

Travis gave Flame's nose one last gentle rub and joined the girls. At the stable, they found Ross grooming one of the ponies.

"Ross, Dana wants to ride," Kim said. "Saddle two ponies for us."

"Please." Dana smiled at Ross.

Kim gave her a startled glance, then looked back at the amused Ross. "Please," she said belatedly.

"Certainly." Ross closed the stall door and went to the tack room. When he returned, he helped the girls saddle the horses, then led them outside to the ring. Travis followed and leaned against the fence.

"Why not let Travis teach you how to ride?" Ross asked. "He caught on quicker than anyone I've ever seen. And with the daily riding he's done—why, he could ride the horses in any show and probably take a prize."

"Really?" Dana beamed, pleased with the praise her brother received.

Travis felt his face flush and hooked his boot heel over the bottom rail, trying to look casual.

"It's okay with me," Kim responded. "Can you jump, too, Travis?"

"Sure," Travis replied, "but Dana'd better get used to riding again before we try jumping."

He took the girls through the same instruction Ross had given him, patiently guiding Dana. After Dana tired,

Kim begged them to watch her take the jumps. Ross grinned, leading out a young horse, already saddled.

"Thought you might like some exercise, too. Take Shama around," he said, handing the reins to Travis.

Ross and Dana watched as Travis and Kim took the lower jumps. Neither moved as Catherine approached and stood beside them, watching.

"Take her through the gymnastic, Travis!" Ross called.

Without looking back, Travis swung Shama around in an easy curve and galloped to the first of the higher jumps. They moved as one, flowing over the jump as smoothly as silk. Ross grinned at Catherine's surprised sound but said nothing. Travis took the next jump with the same ease, then rounded the far edge of the ring and took the final three jumps in quick succession. He brought the horse back to the watchers. His startled gaze took in the third person, who clapped with the others.

"I didn't know you could ride so well, Travis," Catherine said. "Shama usually doesn't respond to strangers."

Travis dismounted awkwardly, losing the gracefulness he had shown on the horse. He mumbled to his aunt, and then led Shama out of the ring and into the stables.

Catherine shrugged and looked at Ross. "I phoned down about Flame. Is he ready?"

"Yes, ma'am." Ross signaled to a nearby groom, who quickly disappeared into the stable. "I sent someone for him as soon as you called."

Travis returned with the groom, who led Flame. He joined Dana and Kim at the fence and watched Catherine mount the horse. Flame danced eagerly as she settled into the tiny saddle and adjusted the reins calmly. Back straight, riding posture perfect, she took the horse around the ring without jumping.

"Getting some of the kinks out of his system," Ross said softly to Travis. "There's a show coming up in a few weeks. Mrs. Shelver hasn't been on him for a while, and he's raring to go."

Travis nodded, watching the horse and rider enviously. They looked picture perfect, straight out of the pages of a show magazine.

At the end of the field, Flame tossed his head and swerved, trying to take a jump. Catherine held him firmly and turned him back.

"Why didn't she just let him jump?" Travis asked.

"That big horse needs a boss or he'll take control," Ross answered. "And without the rider's expert guidance, a horse could get hurt. Anything from a scratch to a broken bone could be the result of a poor jump."

He moved back from the fence and headed for the stables. "It's back to work for me. See you later, kids."

Travis couldn't watch anymore. Although Flame wasn't his, he had felt drawn to the horse. To see him obviously enjoying and responding to his mistress was more than Travis could bear. He headed back to the house.

"Wait up, Travis," Dana called. By the time she and Kim caught up with the long-legged boy, she was almost out of breath. "Slow down! I never get to see you much anymore."

"Sorry." Travis matched his stride to hers. "How about a game of checkers tonight?"

"Sure. It'll have to be after church, though." Dana didn't see his face tighten. "Guess what! Kim and Aunt Emily are going with us."

"How'd you get that past Wade?"

"Aunt Emily said it wasn't easy, but it was worth it. Won't it be fun to have them too, Travis?"

"I'm not going."

Dana stopped and stared at Travis. "Why not?"

"Because I don't want to, that's why!" Travis lengthened his stride and left the girls behind.

That night, after the group left for church, he found himself alone in the big house. Wade and Catherine had gone to a charity dinner, leaving word that they would not return before two o'clock in the morning. Oppressed by the deserted atmosphere of the house, Travis wandered down to the stables. Doors barred, lights off, it also had a deserted appearance. But inside a horse nickered, and another answered.

"I'd rather talk to a horse any day," Travis muttered and unbarred the door. Inside he stopped to speak to each horse, then moved on to Flame's stall. He sat on a bale of hay beside the stall and talked to the horse, voicing his complaints about the way things were in general.

Even he wasn't sure when he actually decided to ride Flame. Usually being with the horses soothed him, but tonight the resentment that simmered within him left him aching and empty. He felt like riding and riding, letting the wind blow away the sick feeling. Abruptly he stood and went to get Flame's tack. "If I'm going to stay in trouble all the time, it might as well be for a good reason," he said as he saddled the horse.

Swinging the barn door wide, he mounted and rode out into the night. The moon shone blue-white against the clear sky, and a cool breeze tugged at Flame's mane. Flame pulled against the bit as they headed out into the pasture.

"Ready to run, boy?" Travis said, leaning forward. "So am I!"

He loosened his grip on the reins, and the big horse jumped forward, breaking into a gallop. For nearly an hour, they raced across the dewy grass. When Travis turned

Flame back toward the stables, both horse and rider had worked the tenseness out of their systems. "How about extra oats, Flame?" he asked, patting him on the neck. Flame whinnied. Travis grinned and touched the horse with his heel.

They galloped up out of a hollow. Just over the rise of ground, Flame stumbled and went down to his knees. Travis landed flat, his breath knocked out of him. When he scrambled to his feet, Flame stood nearby, reins trailing. He stood on three legs.

Fearfully, Travis ran his hands over the slender ankle of the leg Flame kept lifted. Just as he breathed a sigh of relief at finding no breaks, his fingers touched the blood.

"Flame," he said despairingly. "I never meant to hurt you. I never meant to."

Slowly and carefully, he led the limping horse back to the stables. When he passed the house phone, he hesitated, then turned Flame into his stall. In the light, he could see that the cut, though not a break, was bleeding badly. He needed help.

Travis went back to the phone and lifted the receiver. It rang again and again. No one answered. Frantically, he thumbed through the book that dangled beside the telephone. When he dialed Ross's number, a sleepy voice answered.

All sleepiness fled when he heard Travis's stumbled apology. "I'll be right there as soon as I call the vet," he said hastily.

Travis stayed beside Flame. He didn't move even when the vet arrived. Ross let him stay, knowing how he felt. When Emily and the girls returned from church, they saw the lights and drove down. Ross had called the Shelvers. Even Travis understood that Catherine would want to be with Flame. When they arrived, Travis silently gave up his place to his aunt.

Wade spoke for a moment to Ross, then turned to Travis. "Follow me."

By the time they reached the study, Travis had suppressed all emotion and responded woodenly to his uncle. Wade tried to talk calmly, but Travis's lack of response angered him.

"Travis, what is it going to take to make you accept living here? There have been nothing but problems." Wade stood up and walked to the window.

"You can have whatever you want, do whatever you want, and all you do is behave like—well, Travis, what do you want?" Wade faced him with a puzzled frown.

"It's a pity you didn't ask me that four months ago. I told you anyway, but you weren't listening. I wanted to stay on our farm." Travis shut out the thought of Flame. "Since that's no longer an option, what I really want is to be anywhere but here."

Wade's jaw clenched. "Well, you are here."

"Yes. But you can't buy me."

"You might do yourself a favor to make the best of it. You're stuck with us for a while."

"If it weren't for my sisters, I wouldn't be here at all." Travis leaned back in the chair and closed his eyes.

"What would it take to convince you that there are advantages to living here?"

Travis shrugged.

"Is there anything further you want?"

No response.

"Anything I can say? do?" Wade was growing angry. "I feel like I'm catering to a spoiled brat. What is it that you hate about this place so much?"

"Actually, I think it's the people I don't care much for."

Wade's eyes slitted and his voice tightened. "You claim to think so much of your parents. Well, I'll tell you that apparently they were never able to teach you much sense of gratitude, respect, or obedience! In all my days," Wade walked back to the window and jerked the curtain aside to stare down at the stables, "I've never seen such a chip-on-the-shoulder, piously ignorant, hillbilly attitude. If that's what you've inherited from your father—"

Wade whirled as Travis, eyes blazing, leaped up as if he would actually strike his uncle. Tension hung in the room like thick fog. Travis took a step nearer.

"If we're going to start name-calling, I'll start with a few like cheat and liar! Maybe I'd adjust to this family if I could respect the people who live here!"

Wade stared at him. "Go to your room until you've cooled off, young man. I'll deal with you later."

Travis stalked out, anger masking his fear for the horse. Wade Shelver watched him go. Then he sat down and turned the chair toward the dark window. He rubbed his forehead to ease the tension and waited.

When Catherine entered, he stood up and walked quickly across the room. "How is he?" he asked.

"He'll be lame for a while, but he'll be all right. It could have been a lot worse." She tried to brush dirt from the hem of her gown, then gave up and sat down across from him.

"What did you do about Travis?"

"Nothing yet." Wade sat back down wearily. "It's a pity he's not more like his sisters. Kim, Dana, and Laurie seem to get along. Maybe I just don't know how to handle boys."

"That may be part of it," Catherine admitted, "but certainly not all. Perhaps he needs more discipline than we can give. The Warners were telling me about their son. They had to send him to Ashleigh Military Academy. Maybe that's the answer for Travis."

"I don't know—"

"We just can't let him continually upset the entire family. We have to do something."

"I'll talk to Laurie in the morning. Then Travis."

CHAPTER ELEVEN
THE STRANGER

The next morning, Travis wandered aimlessly around the stable area until Ross finally insisted he keep an eye on Flame. Settling on a nearby bale of straw, Travis watched the gelding. Tall, graceful, and long-limbed, Flame was the exact opposite of the blocky little sprinters that Travis had grown up around. He found more differences every time he looked, yet there was something in the gelding's cat-like grace that reminded Travis of the short-coupled, fleet Winsome.

He had no idea how much time passed. Eventually, Travis's stomach told him it was nearly dinnertime. He didn't want to eat with the Shelvers, but, thinking of Laurie and Dana, he pushed reluctantly off the bale.

As he left the stable, Travis noted with idle curiosity that a stranger stood in the driveway, beside a jeep-wagon, talking with Ross. Travis put his hand on the post of a paddock fence to aid himself in jumping over. As his indifferent gaze focused on the man beside the vehicle, his hand tightened into a savage grip on the fence.

Heedless of the splinters pushing into his hand, Travis held the grip. It suddenly seemed to be the only steady thing in his life. His face turned a white that rivaled the fence itself, his eyes wide and disbelieving. Travis could hear his own heart pounding, and the blood roaring in his ears.

A weanling colt, curious at the boy's stillness, stepped cautiously in his direction, only to scramble away as Travis leaped over the fence in a single move. He walked quickly—almost ran—to the two men.

They fell silent as he approached. To Travis, the ground at his feet seemed to spin as he stared at the man before him. The man stood well over six feet, big and broad. Even in mid-November, his face was darkly tanned—if a little haggard. His calloused hands spoke silently of hard work, in the not-too-distant past. The man's face held Travis's wondering gaze. The dark blue eyes, bright and questioning, searched Travis thoroughly. The stranger was crowned with a thick crop of dark red hair—the identical color of Travis's own, except that it was mixed with grey at the sides.

"Hello, Travis." The stranger spoke at last. "Travis, Jr., I believe?"

"You're my Uncle James!" The words burst from Travis. "Everyone thought you were dead . . . they have for years and years. We thought you were killed in the war—"

"Travis." James McLarren's laughter checked his nephew's spluttering. He reached out to fold the boy in strong arms. "I'm glad to see you, too. And I want to tell you and the others all about it. Is your Uncle Wade about?"

"Why him?" Travis began angrily. "What does he have to do with anything?"

James met Travis's eyes calmly. "Just about everything, I guess. I'd like to have permission to visit my nieces and nephew."

"But—" Travis broke off and flushed deeply as his uncle shook his head and frowned. "Yes, sir," he finished.

James turned back to Ross. "Like I said, I need to see Wade Shelver."

"I'll see to that right away, if you want to come with me." Ross beckoned James to follow him, and Travis followed his newfound uncle. Travis was strangely disoriented; everything felt either too far away, too near, too loud, or too quiet to be realistic. Like swimming underwater, he thought.

Emily met them in the hall as they tramped in, single file. "Where's Mr. Shelver?" Ross asked, without preamble.

"He's in the office with Laurie, but I really don't think you'd better—" she stopped and blanched white as she saw McLarren. "Travis!—No, of course not. You must be his brother. . . ."

"James," he supplied, nodding his head. They stopped while Ross went into the office hall, walked straight to the double oak doors, and knocked.

"Later!" the curt reply came instantly. Ross called back.

"Mr. Shelver? This is Ross, and I really think you'd like to meet your visitor." A moment of silence followed, then the doors swung open. Wade strode out.

"What's going—" He broke off abruptly when he saw McLarren. For a long moment not one person so much as breathed.

Then James stepped forward, hand outstretched. "I'm Travis's brother, James."

"Well. James McLarren," Wade finally said slowly. "So Vietnam didn't carry you away after all."

"No, I was a prisoner of war. Not dead. It's taken me a while to straighten everything out and track down the kids."

Wade's gaze went to Travis and around to Laurie, who stood in the office doorway, her white face accentuating tear streaks. Travis stared at her. The problems of yesterday rushed back into his mind. What had Uncle Wade done to her?

When Wade spoke again, it was with quiet challenge. "The children are my wards, McLarren. Unchallengeably and irrevocably."

"As much as it may surprise you, Mr. Shelver, I'm not here to challenge that. I give you my word, before them and before you, that I'm not here to cause trouble. Right now I'm simply asking for the chance to visit with my brother's children."

Wade Shelver was obviously surprised. He stepped forward gingerly, as though he expected the hand to leap out and strike him dead, but he extended his own to James. What followed was not exactly a handshake, but at least was a brief clasp.

"If you will join us for dinner, perhaps we could talk then."

"Of course, thank you."

Wade turned to Travis, who drew his head back and stepped nearer to Laurie. Both men recognized the gesture of defiance. Wade's eyes narrowed. James frowned again with puzzled disapproval.

"Travis, go get Dana. Tell her we're ready to eat." Glancing at Laurie, Wade continued on a gentler note. "Go ahead and get cleaned up for dinner. I think we've said all that we need to say."

Travis and Laurie left the room quickly. Once alone upstairs, Travis grabbed Laurie's arm. "What is going on with you two?"

"Oh, Travis," Laurie's tears started afresh. "He's going to send you away!"

"He's *what?*"

"Uncle Wade and Aunt Catherine think you're irresponsible and need discipline. Oh, Travis, he's going to talk to you after dinner. I shouldn't tell you, but if you would only get hold of yourself and talk to him properly, maybe he wouldn't send you to that school. Please, Travis!"

"What good could I do? He's made up his mind to get rid of me and that's that. You'll probably be next! He'll split up the whole family, what's left of it."

"He won't do that to us." Laurie turned pleading eyes to Travis.

"Just like we thought he couldn't make us leave the farm, huh?" Travis laughed bitterly. "Laurie, the only reason I came to this place was so we could all be together. Now, over my dead body is he going to send me off to, to—"

"West Virginia," she finished sadly. "Boarding school."

"Virginia, baloney. We'll think of something. But right now, we have to get down there before someone has to come looking for us. You go do whatever it is you have to. I'll get Dana."

She just leaned against the wall and stared at him hopelessly, one hand holding her hair back from her forehead.

"Go on," he urged. "I'll meet you back here and we'll go together. Maybe Uncle James can help."

Travis turned and ran downstairs to the library. "Dana!" he called. "Dana! Come on to dinner, and hurry up! It's important!"

CHAPTER TWELVE
TWO UNCLES

Less than ten minutes later, everyone had gathered in the dining room. Travis could hardly contain his excitement as he sat in his usual chair. The tension flowed around the table in waves. Travis earned a disapproving glare from his Aunt Catherine when he dropped his napkin. He just couldn't keep his mind on dinner.

Finally, after prompting from Emily, James McLarren plunged into his story. Very quickly, the whole table was caught up in James's sketch of the five years he had spent in a prison camp; his escape; the other months it had taken him, moving when he could and hiding when he couldn't, to make his way out of Communist territory on foot; his reunion with his wife, Beth; and the time in rehabilitation, before the doctors would permit them to return to the United States.

"So, you see," James paused to chew thoughtfully, "I've really only been back in the States for a couple of weeks. When Beth and I got back, we found the letters you had written, and one from the Rallerts. Beth had kept in touch with Travis and Grace through the years, though she had moved away."

"What about the farm?" Dana piped up. "Didn't you want to go home?"

"Well, Dana, that's the first place we went after we read the letters. The farm had been bulldozed, of course, but we visited the Rallerts."

Travis thought about Winsome and almost interrupted Uncle James but thought better of it.

Uncle James continued, "They told us everything we needed to know. Then the next thing I wanted to do was to come and see you and Travis and Laurie." James turned his attention back to the rest of the group.

"How did you find us?" Laurie asked.

"Well, it wasn't difficult, really." He put down his fork and looked at her. "I was here in Asheville for your folks' wedding. I'd never been to Chellavue, but it wasn't hard to find. The Shelver name is well known here."

"And now that you have everything straightened out," Emily asked, "what do you plan to do?"

"My wife and I are making our permanent home in Fairmont." James laid his napkin down and propped his elbows on the table. "I have a little catching up with life to do."

"Fairmont." Wade came into the conversation. "Well, now, that is interesting. Ashleigh Military Academy is located in Fairmont."

"Really?" James looked puzzled. "A boarding school?"

"Yes," Wade continued, as Laurie concentrated on her food. "We've decided that Ashleigh might meet some of our needs for a while."

James opened his mouth, then closed it again. His gaze traveled from Laurie's pale face to the open hostility and anger in Travis's. Finally, James responded carefully.

"Ashleigh Academy is less than forty miles from my home. Would you object to my wife and I visiting the children? Or even, I'm sure you know that they would be welcome to stay with us."

Travis tightened his grip on his fork. Why don't we all just go there? he thought. He had to bite his tongue to keep from saying the words aloud.

"The plans have not been finalized," Wade said, looking at Travis. "We'll discuss your invitation later."

"As you wish. Just so long as you both realize any of the children would be welcome in our home."

Travis felt his Uncle James' eyes on him, but would not look up to meet them.

Fortunately, Dana chose that moment to join the discussion. "Are you ever going to come and visit us here?"

Travis pounced on that. "Probably not, Dana. Uncle Wade wouldn't want him to."

"And why wouldn't I want him to?" Wade's voice was deadly calm.

"Well," Travis took a long drink of water and set his glass down with a thump. "Uncle James is a lot like Dad. And you didn't like Dad too much, did you?"

James McLarren's eyebrows shot up. For the first time he looked really angry at his nephew.

"James will be welcome to visit here any time he wishes to do so."

"Do you mind if I take you up on that Saturday?" James asked. "I would like to bring my wife back to see the kids."

"Of course."

"Well, we'll be along after breakfast, then, if that's all right."

Wade nodded. Emily began asking James further questions about his wife and plans for the future, effectively blocking Travis from any further opportunity to cause a disagreement. He was left to glower through the remainder of the meal.

Travis's mind was scrambling with plans to keep his family together. He felt sure James would help, if he could just get him alone to explain the situation.

Tonight obviously wasn't the time. He would catch him Saturday when he came back.

CHAPTER THIRTEEN
RUNNING OUT OF TIME

Though Travis knew that Wade intended to send him to the Academy, Wade made it official during a family conference. Travis stubbornly refused to listen to Laurie or to Dana when they begged him to yield to his uncle. The meeting had ended in a stalemate. For Travis, the days ticked by slowly as he waited for a chance to enlist Uncle James on his side.

Saturday morning he leaned against the fence and watched Catherine lead Flame along slowly. She was working the big chestnut in the field near the road, exercising the damaged foreleg. Travis stayed where he was and watched, still feeling guilty about hurting the horse. Besides, he knew that James McLarren would return momentarily, and he had no intentions of letting him get to the house before talking with him.

Flame tired of the walking routine and nickered at Travis. Catherine dismounted and led him over to Travis.

"He likes you a lot, I see," she said, watching him uneasily.

Travis looked at Flame and nodded, swallowing hard. "I didn't mean to hurt him," he said quickly.

"I can see that," Catherine said, watching Flame nuzzle the boy. "You have a way with horses. If only—"

She broke off. "I have some telephone calls to make. Would you walk him for a while, then take him back to the stables?"

"Sure!"

Catherine watched him for a moment and then, satisfied, went back to the house. Travis kept Flame moving along the fence. Finally, a familiar-looking jeep wagon came into view. As it slowed down to make the turn into Chellavue, Travis led Flame toward the road. Opening a fence, he walked the horse outside. James stopped the jeep and climbed out.

"Hey, there!" James called. "That's some horse! You must have done a lot of riding since you've been here."

Travis flinched. "Well, a little more than I should have. I never rode jumpers until I came here."

"Come on over here and see if you remember my wife," James beckoned. Travis led Flame forward. He peered in the driver's door to see a tall brunette woman on the other side.

She leaned across the seat and spoke before either James or Travis did. "Hi, Travis." Her voice was warm and eager. "It's so nice to see you again! I can't tell you how I've looked forward to it!"

"Hi, Aunt Beth! It's sure good to see you all, too. You'll never know how good."

Beth laughed. "And that is simply a beautiful horse! Could you be bribed into letting me ride with you sometime?"

Travis grinned. "Sure!" But the grin quickly disappeared. "Uncle James?" Travis lowered his voice. "I wanted to ask you something."

"Okay, ask."

"Well. . . ."

"Oh, I see. Privately. Right?" At Travis's nod, James glanced briefly at his wife. She settled back in her seat and smiled.

James followed Travis as he led Flame to the other side of the driveway. Travis allowed Flame to start cropping the short grass.

"I was hoping," Travis began, "that you might have some idea of how we can get out of this mess. I'm the one they're going to ship off like an old package."

"I sort of thought that's what you were going to say," James smiled. "Really, Travis, I'm not sure exactly how to say this, because I want to help you kids in any way I can." James absently ran his hand over Flame's back. "I'm not really sure that there's anything I can do, and I'm not really sure that I would be right in interfering with this family anyway—having just walked in on you."

"We are not a family!" Travis's eyes flashed as he spoke. "My family is my sisters. Not them!"

James was taken aback by the outburst. "Travis, I hope you consider them your family. You do live here, and they are your aunt and uncle—just as Beth and I are. Does that mean that you don't consider me family either?"

"You're different."

"How?"

"They took our home away! They ruined everything! Do you know what he did—"

"Yes, Travis. I know. Wade told me the whole story."

"Okay, then. That land was as much yours as ours! Doesn't it bother you at all?"

"I *was* unhappy that the farm was sold—"

"All right—"

"Travis! I won't change what's done. Your sisters have adjusted well here, and I'm not going to get into a battle with the courts and upset things. Travis, nothing in the past is an excuse for wrong attitudes or actions now! I know you grew up in a Christian family, Travis." James paused for a long time. "What do you think your father would say about the way you view the Shelvers?"

"He never made us associate with them before, and I wish we didn't have to now."

"But he did pray for them, and he would never have condoned disrespect."

"They don't deserve respect. They're not even honest."

"Travis, God's word commands us to respect those in legal authority over us. Check Romans 13."

Travis pulled Flame's head up. "Does all this mean you're going to help us or not?"

"Of course I'll help you, Travis. But not by interfering with your legal guardian."

Travis stared at him, anger showing plainly in his eyes. James met his gaze unflinchingly. With no further comment, Travis led Flame back through the gate and across the pasture, forcing himself to walk slowly for Flame's benefit.

James returned to his seat in the jeep wagon. "Well," Beth questioned, "what was that all about?"

"Just what I expected, really." The big man leaned back in his seat. "He hates it here, and he expects me to jump in and take his part."

Beth was silent.

"I must admit it's a temptation," James continued. "Travis needs something that he's not going to get from Wade. He's openly rebellious." James shook his head. "I wish you could have seen him the other day. He doesn't care who knows what he thinks of the Shelvers. In fact, I think the more people that know, the happier he is."

Beth laughed. "He's headstrong. Just like his daddy. And his uncle."

"Seems like if that's true, I should have some better idea how to snap him out of it." He shrugged and started the engine.

Travis stayed at the barn with Flame. Lunch time came and went.

Finally, taking pains to avoid everyone, Travis circled the house and entered through the kitchen-hall door. Slipping quietly upstairs, Travis went to Laurie's room. He peered up and down the hall before knocking cautiously on the door.

"Where have you been?" Laurie demanded, when she opened the door. "You're not exactly winning extra points with Aunt Catherine by skipping out on meals while there's company here."

"I don't really care what she thinks. I wasn't in the mood for our company. We already had our conversation for the day."

"Oh?"

"Yeah." Travis pushed himself away from the window and began pacing around the room. "I tried to get Uncle James to help us, Laurie, and he said no. Just flat, plain no. Laurie, do you want me to go?"

"Of course not! I mean—I don't want us to be separated." She thought for a minute, then said, "Travis, as long as I know I'm doing what's right, I believe that God will put me where He wants me to be. I have to be content with whatever that is. I'm praying that you will find that contentment too. God knows what's best for me, and for you, too."

"So what Dana and I want doesn't matter either, right?"

"No, not really. Not when it cuts across what the Lord wants!"

"I hope you don't ever expect me to be 'content' with something that makes us all miserable!"

"Travis, you know better than what you're saying! Are you ever going to quit being so bullheaded that you think you know better than God?" She squared her shoulders and looked him straight in the eye. "Mom and Dad would be ashamed of you and the way you've acted!"

"So you want me to quit? Just like you?" Travis turned to face her.

"Travis, I think you'd better just get out of here for now, or I think I'm going to say something I'll regret." Her eyes spilled over with tears. "I've done everything I could think of to try to keep you and Dana together and happy. You've done nothing but whine and complain for months! Now just leave! Please."

A long second passed. Travis turned and left without a backward glance. Pausing in the hall, he felt tears burning in his own eyes. Angrily brushing them away, he fought the impulse to return to his sister's room.

Instead, Travis sought refuge in the deserted library. He lay flopped on a large sofa, staring at the intricate woodwork of the ceiling. Voices and footsteps circled around and around in the big house. Travis, his mind awhirl, didn't try to keep track of them. He was only vaguely aware of their presence until they ceased altogether. He was about to push himself up to investigate when Dana appeared in the door.

"Come on, Travis," she said. "Aren't you going to at least say good-bye to Uncle James and Aunt Beth?"

Travis rolled his eyes up. "What a mess," he whispered. He felt the tears threatening to return. "What a rotten mess!"

"You're being awfully nasty." Dana's voice was decided and firm. "Daddy would tan you good."

"Hush, Dana!" Travis bounced to his feet. "I don't want to hear any more!"

"Any more of what?" Dana cut in with an aggressive tilt to her chin.

"Everyone expects this whole mess to work out just *perfectly!* Well, you're all crazy! So if you know what's good for you, just get out of here!"

Dana didn't look afraid. "What's the matter, Travis? Don't you think Jesus knows what He's doing?"

"Hush, Dana! Just hush!"

She gave him a measuring look. "You're acting like a baby. I guess I'll have to tell them good-bye for you." She turned and disappeared. Travis heard her hurried footsteps growing fainter down the hall.

CHAPTER FOURTEEN
WHAT NOW?

"First Laurie, then Uncle James, and now Dana!" Travis fumed as he left Chellavue and headed down the road toward town. Feeling more than a little deserted by his sisters and his Uncle James, Travis stubbornly tried to hold on to his anger. But by the time he reached the little church Laurie and Dana had been attending, he found himself confused and alone. Unable to reach out to the family, he sought the only other source of help he knew.

Travis slowly climbed the wooden steps of the church. Moving into the shadow of the porch, he reached for the door handle. Locked! Tears still stung Travis's eyes. "Typical," he muttered. "He's never been there yet when I needed Him. Why now?"

The boy turned to leave, but felt the tears of frustration threatening to take over again. He wasn't about to go back to the house. Sliding down with his back against the church door, he folded his arms on his knees and studied the sky.

His voice came as a whisper. "I don't believe Mom and Dad could have been completely wrong." His fingers tightened on the denim of his jeans. "But, God, if You're true, why aren't You ever real to me, like You were to them?"

A cricket started a rhythmic chirping somewhere in the hedges around the porch. A cool breeze ruffled the leaves in the trees, but Travis heard no thunderclap to answer his question. Suddenly footsteps sounded on the far end of the porch. One swift motion brought Travis to his feet. He faced the approaching figure, instantly defensive, until he saw that it was Pastor Riordan. Then he turned to leave.

"I'm sorry," Travis mumbled. "I wasn't hurting anything. I just needed somewhere to think."

"I know you weren't hurting anything, Travis." The pastor put out a hand to stop him. "Please don't go. I just heard a noise and thought someone might need something. I didn't know it was you."

Pastor Riordan sat down on the steps. "I've prayed that God would give me a chance to talk to you."

"Why does it always work for everyone but me?" Travis said, as he kicked a step with his toe.

"Why does what work?"

Travis whirled around and struck the railing a hard blow. "They're sending me away!" The tears tried to take over again. "They're sending me away, and I can't do a thing about it!" His words came in a rush.

"I know," said the pastor quietly. "Laurie called and told me."

"You know! Then why couldn't you say one of your prayers to do something about it?"

"God is not a vending machine, Travis. Prayer is a means we have of working with God, not of getting Him to cater to our own interests. Don't you believe that He has reasons for allowing this to happen?"

"Oh, yes! The famous line! 'It's God's will.' " Travis mimicked. "Laurie, Dana, you." His voice was losing strength. "What is it that everyone but me sees? If this is God's will, I think it's a pretty lousy will! Mom and Dad died months ago, and I have yet to see one good thing come of it. What is it? I mean, why—"

Travis stopped completely. He sank to the steps, burying his face in his hands. At last, genuine sobs shook his body.

Pastor Riordan waited a long time before he answered. "Do you really want to know what 'it' is, Travis?"

The red head nodded silently, and then Travis spoke in a barely audible voice. "I grew up in the same family. I thought I believed the same things about God, but I just can't see. . . ."

"Travis, do you believe in God?"

"I guess I believe He's there. Somewhere. Just never there for me."

"Knowing your parents as well as I did, I know they must have told you about how Christ came to earth to die on the cross for our sins."

"Yes! I thought I believed that, too. I mean, I know it's true, but it always seems so much more real to everyone else."

"Have you ever come to the point where you, personally, accepted what the Lord did for you?"

Travis looked down. "I'm not sure. At least, I don't think so now."

"Have you ever read Psalm 139? 'Thine eyes did see my substance, yet being unperfect; and in thy book all my members were written . . . when as yet there was none of them.' Travis, before you were ever born, God knew all about you. Before He came to earth to die, He knew that you would be sitting on this porch tonight. He knew every wrong thing you were ever going to do."

Travis gave a twisted smile. "I guess that's been plenty, lately."

Pastor Riordan smiled, too. "But, you see, Travis, even knowing all that, Christ still came down here to pay the price for those sins. 'God commendeth His love toward us in that while we were yet sinners, Christ died for us.'"

Travis was silent.

"He offers forgiveness for those sins as a free gift. But there must come a point where you realize that you can never straighten out your life on your own. Then, if you ask Him, He will take over your sins and bring peace to your heart about all that's troubling you now, Travis. But you must admit your helplessness and ask."

Travis nodded.

"You've never done that, have you?"

"No." The answer was a whisper. "But you're right. Everything is too big of a mess—and most of it is my own fault."

"Surrender to Him, Travis. Ask His forgiveness."

Travis nodded, and bowed his head.

An hour later, Travis was walking slowly toward Chellavue. The familiar knots of tension were gone. He could breathe freely for the first time in weeks. He knew that the battle he had been fighting was over—and that he'd found the answer to his question.

"I finally know at least one reason we had to move down here," Travis spoke aloud. He thought back to his life on the farm, and wondered if he ever would have realized his need for Christ if he had stayed there. Suddenly the thought hit Travis with a nearly physical impact— God had even used his Uncle Wade to bring Travis where he needed to be! "If we'd stayed on the farm. . . ." Travis's

voice was almost a whisper. "Well, I guess now I just wait to see what the Lord has planned. And from now on, I won't fight it!"

Laurie's words echoed in his head. *"I'm content in the way that matters the most, Travis."*

"Yeah, Laurie," Travis smiled. "I know what you mean. Hey!" Travis stopped in his tracks, speaking aloud. "I'm going to see Mom and Dad again!"

The late-evening stillness was shattered by an exultant Cherokee war whoop. A startled cat, slinking through the bushes, froze as he watched a red-headed boy turn a running handspring and take off down the road.

CHAPTER FIFTEEN

UNDERSTANDING AT LAST

Travis walked up the driveway to Chellavue. His thoughts were running back over the time since he had come to live here. Travis felt his face burn at the memories.

Then he leaned on the fence, not even noticing the horses that had been his only comfort these last months. "Dear Lord," he prayed, "I haven't really done much right since I've been here. But I have You to help me now. Oh God, I need Your help! Let me know what to say."

Travis found his uncle in the study. At the other desk, Catherine sat thumbing through a desk calendar. She stopped and looked at Travis uneasily. Wade glanced up, anger coming immediately to his eyes. Travis took a quick breath and plunged in. "I know you're angry, and I don't blame you. You have every right to be."

Wade's eyebrows shot up. Without moving, he continued to stare at Travis.

"I want to talk to you. To both of you, if I may."

Wade gave a single nod. "Sit down, Travis."

Travis sat on the edge of his seat and leaned forward. Licking his lips nervously, he began, "Sir, I owe you a really big apology."

Wade didn't reply, but his eyes never left Travis's face. Catherine put her pencil down slowly.

"You were right about one thing," Travis continued. "I have been disrespectful and ungrateful. But I didn't learn it from my parents!" Travis's voice contained just a hint of its old vehemence. "They taught me better. But God had to take them from me before I'd be willing to learn some lessons." Travis paused and gripped the arms of the chair. "And they used to pray for you all the time.

"Uncle Wade, I have to be honest. I still don't like what you've done, and I believe you're wrong. You sold our farm without our permission, and you've used the money for your own ends. But that was no excuse for me to act like I have. Things will be different, because tonight I asked God to forgive me—and He's shown me how wrong I was."

Wade seemed to have trouble finding his voice. "Well, Travis, I'm not really sure I know what to say to you. I don't really understand what's going on. I knew you were angry about the sale of the farm, but I never realized that you thought I was stealing your money."

"I heard you and that lawyer discussing your investments."

Wade thought for a minute. "Oh, that." A wry grin twisted Wade's lips. "If you had listened a little longer, you would have discovered that the benefactors of that investment are you children. All the money is in the trust fund—the money from the sale of the farm, the profit we made from the investment—everything. You can see the books if you like."

"Then why didn't you tell us?"

"Well, you were so angry at me. I wanted to avoid another confrontation. I don't like being called a thief, you know. And if you hadn't overheard, no harm would have been done. As it is. . . ." He hesitated. "About the Academy, Travis. . . ."

"I'll go, if that is what you decide." Travis swallowed. "I realize now that the Lord has a reason for everything that He allows in our lives . . . , and He allowed you in my life." Travis's direct look lacked its old defiant challenge. "So I intend to make the best of it. Maybe someday you'll realize you need God too."

Wade looked away, and his voice grew thoughtful. "Ironic. Those are the last words that I ever heard your mother say."

Travis glanced at him sharply.

"Grace used to call about once a month. Maybe you knew that. She always told Emily that she was praying that somehow I would realize I needed God just like anyone else."

"It's true, you know."

"Could be. Anything that would quiet your tongue could be worth thinking about." Wade half smiled to take the sting out of his words. Then he leaned back in the chair, a troubled look returning to his face. When he spoke again, he chose his words carefully. "But about the Academy . . . if there is any way that we can work things out. . . ."

Catherine glanced at him, then at Travis. "He's certainly good with the horses, Wade. Perhaps if he could train them, show them for Chellavue, it would give him a purpose here."

Travis could scarcely breathe. "You could say that after I hurt Flame?"

"I know you didn't mean to hurt Flame. Everything was in such a turmoil, and perhaps all of it wasn't your fault."

She stood up and walked across the room to lean on Wade's desk. "You three have taught me a thing or two since you've been here. Laurie has been such a help that I've actually had free time to spend with Kim."

Catherine paused to glance back at Wade. "I honestly didn't realize how much I had been neglecting her. And I'm finding that I don't know how to answer her questions about—well, about church."

She looked at Travis thoughtfully. "If this change of yours continues, we might actually make a family here. What do you think, Wade?"

Wade let out his breath in a sigh of relief. Getting up, he walked around to Travis. "All right, we'll give it a try. To tell the truth, I was miserable at the thought of throwing one of Grace's children out, so to speak. It was almost like going through the whole mess again. I was wrong then, and I'll be glad to be proved wrong again."

"I'd enjoy doing it, sir."

Both Wade and Catherine smiled, a little ruefully. "I'm sure you would, Travis," Wade said, "but for now, it's late. You'd better get to bed."

"Yes, sir."

When Travis entered his room, he found Laurie and Dana curled up on his bed. Laurie looked up quickly, then moved as Dana stirred sleepily. "We were worried about you, Travis. What happened?"

"I talked to the pastor, Laurie. Like you say, I accepted Jesus as my Saviour. Now I understand about your contentment."

Laurie leaped off the bed to throw her arms around her brother, dislodging Dana. Blinking, Dana stared at her laughing brother and sister. "What're we celebrating?" she asked sleepily.

"Travis's new birthday," Laurie said happily. "Travis got saved tonight!"

Dana shrieked and joined the other two. "And now you can stay with us?"

"Hold on, Dana," Travis said, sobering down. "That doesn't necessarily follow. I've been a rat lately, suspecting Uncle Wade of anything and everything. But I apologized and promised to straighten up. I think I'll get to stay, but nothing's really settled yet."

"Oh, you will, you will," Dana insisted. "We prayed about it."

Travis looked at Laurie. "All things do work together for good, Laurie. Oh, I still don't see why Mom and Dad had to die."

"I don't either," Laurie said softly. "But being reunited with her family was Mom's prayer. She couldn't do it. We can do it for her. It won't be easy, Travis, you know that."

"I know. I certainly have a lot to live down," he said earnestly. "And in the morning, I'm going to talk to Aunt Emily and call Uncle James and Aunt Beth. They deserve some apologies, too."

And he needed to talk to Ross, and Brad, and the other boys at school. . . . Travis's thoughts raced ahead to tomorrow, to a new day.